TO MY TWO-LEGGED AND FOUR LEGGED BROTHERS AND
SISTERS WHO MAY BE PHYSICALLY, MENTALLY, EMOTIONALLY
AND, OR SPIRITUALLY CHALLENGED.

Press on. Be courageous.

Published by BusyB Creative, Chicago, IL

ISBN-13: 978-1500836306

"Come to the edge."
"We can't. We're afraid."
"Come to the edge."
"We can't. We will fall!"
"Come to the edge."
And they came.
And he pushed them.

—Guillaume Apiollinaire

Prologue

PAUL PHILLECROIX SURELY WOULD have been asphyxiated if he hadn't broken through the last and final layer when he did. His arrival to the world was announced by a blood curdling scream that pierced an opening in the pre-dawn light when he cried out, "Mère?!!" Où êtes-vous mère?!"

The next sound to be heard was that of a meadowlands' reed snapping as it yielded to the weight of Paul Phillecroix' oversized and powerful body.

The love and comfort that Paul Phillecroix was searching for was long gone, but that didn't stop him from crying out for hours and hours until the light slipped past the day and the frogs, crickets and other unknown creatures spoke through the dark of the night keeping Paul in a hushed panic.

It's still a mystery as to whom Paul's parents were and what drove them to leave their newborn to fend for himself in such a thick and lush marshland. And if it wasn't strange enough that the newborn was left on his own, Paul Phillecroix was emblazoned with a bright blue streak. Starting at the top of his neck, it spilled down and through his thick and barrel like chest and came to an abrupt stop at the base of his belly. The *Phillecroix Streak*, as it would come to be known throughout the world, put great demands upon that of its bearer.

The Phillecroix family history has been passed down generation to generation in oral tradition and now resides with its sole heir. No one knows to this day why or how the family's nom de guerre, the brilliant blue streak came to be. What is known, or so legend has it, is that during his first cold, hungry and frightening night alone something spoke to Paul Phillecroix with a voice as pure and light as a Mayfly's wing.

The message, or maybe it was a command, floated in and down through the narrow canal of his tiny ear and created enough momentum and might for Monsieur to vacate his grassy nest. In an unprecedented five days' time from the exact moment he was born, Paul Phillecroix took flight from what King Louis XVI would one day deem the most beautiful place on earth and headed for Paris.

The miles of wingspan that separated Paul Phillecroix from Pipio Pibionem are unknown. Pipio's qualities were rare; she was one in a million. She possessed many but having the perfect aerodynamic body was what she used to her advantage most, both on and above the ground. The shape of her distal wings gave her enormous thrust for takeoff along with the ability to soar long distances. Her form also had the unintentional effect of attracting a lot of attention from male suitors. Gentleman birds from all over the world had a Pipio Pibionem-like vision in their heads when they fantasized about their future brides. Many young males spent sleepless nights dreaming and fantasizing about Pipio and her subtly sashaying tail. With glassy eyes they peered through cracks in grass nests late at night and wondered if the crown feathers of their future brides would glisten in the late afternoon sun in the same mesmerizing way as mademoiselle Pibionem's once did. It was enough to keep an excited young bird up all night and the females of the flock in a jealous rage.

To keep Pipio safe from lurking eyes and clawing claws,

Pipio's father connected with his connections and arranged for her to fly and flock with the famous D'Artagnan of Gascony. Not much needs to be said about D'Artagnan except that he was a pioneer of his time and was responsible for the development of the first organized pigeon flight paths.

The year 1785 sent Pipio east to Brittany as part of a habitat and flying experiment on behalf of her new mentor, D'Artagnan. D'Artagnan was testing his theory that fellow pigeons had the ability to fly long distances and return to the exact latitude and longitude from where they embarked. D'Artagnan wanted to prove and record the results of sending birds long distances tracing their way back to where they started. D'Artagnan also set out to prove the unconscious process that he and others like him would use to chart the skies they fly and then relay their coordinates to any bird of any color at any time.

No one knows what D'Artagnan must have been thinking or feeling the day he encouraged his young charge, Pipio, to take to the air and watched her fly into the sunset never to return. A dejected D'Artagnan waited for days on end without food, water or sleep until his legs buckled and he froze to death on the granite coast.

Pipio did return to her point of embarkation just hours after D'Artagnan perished, feathers and bones cracked by the icy air. She wasn't alone. Joining her was a young, strong and handsome bird that had an unusual and yet distinguishable bright blue streak running down his chest. Six months later in the Norman town of Vattetot-sous-Beaumont near the English Channel, Pipio Pibionem married Paul Phillecroix I. Their meeting had been designed in the heavens, painted with bright and passionate colors. As it turned out, Pipio and Paul met when their flight paths crossed - he was traveling from the east and she from the west. At six hundred feet, the young and dashing Paul Phillecroix I dipped his wing to Pipio and said, "Vous êtes beau! I shall follow her tail if she'll allow me the pleasure." Paul's wish to trail Pipio's tail feathers was quickly granted when the mortified Pipio fell flush and went into a tailspin sending her straight to the concrete waters below. Paul went after her like a speeding bullet and clutched her in his claws just inches from the water's crust. As they ascended from the watery grave, blood rushed to Pipio's head and the usually reticent mademoiselle Pibionem let fall from her beak, "C'est l'amour."

Yes, it was love and not long after their wedding Pipio gave birth to a daughter and she and her slightly disappointed husband Paul, who had hoped for a son, named the young squab, Penelope Phillecroix.

Following the birth of Penelope, Paul's wish for a son was granted when Pipio delivered Paul Phillecroix II. He was much like his father: strong, powerful and handsome. A lot of expectations were thrust upon young Paul, not the least, carrying on the Phillecroix name and tradition of flying excellence. Paul Phillecroix II eventually had the opportunity to bear the pride of his family on each wing when he became the youngest pigeon ever to pilot himself to the South Pole and back in twenty-nine days. Upon his return he was showered with affection and admiration from flocks across Europe. At the end of the reception line was a young and beautiful bird named Agnès Amalric. Paul Phillecroix II immediately swept her off her pretty pink feet and they soared into the setting sun. Not long after their marriage was consummated another Phillecroix was born and was named Paul Phillecroix III.

The third Paul Phillecroix was hatched on a warm and sunlit day much like his great grandfather before him. And like his great grandfather, his mettle was tested early on a blustery day in March 1815. Young Paul Phillecroix III was summoned by France's highest military authority to deliver news to Napoleon Bonaparte who was recently exiled to the island of Elba in the Mediterranean Sea. Paul successfully flew the seven hundred sixty-five miles non-stop from Paris in order to relay a message from Napoleon's beloved wife the Archduchess of Habsburg, Marie Louise. Marie Louise, who was sick and tired of spending countless nights alone while little Napoleon was out conquering the world, insisted that he escape at once, go to the patisserie and bring home her favorite chocolate croissants. "Napo," as Marie Louise referred to Napoleon, quickly scribbled a note notifying Marie Louise that her sweet and flaky confections would have to wait as he was headed for Belgium. He then tied the note to Paul's left leg and threw him skyward.

M. Phillecroix made the return trip to Paris in the record-breaking time of twenty-three hours, five minutes. Although Paul Phillecroix III's time was quite impressive, he would have actually completed the trip much more quickly had not his fancy been tickled by an athletic looking gal named Theresa Morin. Theresa, who came from impressive stock, was the by product of a mother and father who were also employed by Napoleon to deliver messages to his league of fighters during the Revolution. Paul Phillecroix III was immediately smitten with Theresa's innate sense of courage and honesty. The pair of lovebirds sealed their devotion and soon after Theresa Morin gave birth to Paul Phillecroix IV.

Long before Amelia Earhart made her historic transatlantic journey, Piette Delacroix, a distant blood relative to Pipio Pibionem, completed the reverse flight in twenty-four hours with a stop-over in London. On a warm spring day in 1933 Piette left her rooftop perch in Paris with a request strapped to her thin left leg. Addressed to President Roosevelt it began, "Monsieur, s'il vous plaît, please send more of those delicious biscuits that my wife and I so thoroughly enjoyed when you were here last." It was signed by the then Prime Minister of France, Albert-Pierre Sarraut.

The last daring and heroic flight from the now famous Phillecroix family of pigeons occurred on June 3, 1947 when Paul

Phillecroix V the offspring of Paul Phillecroix IV and his wife Alexandria completed an around-the-world trip in just under two weeks' time. What's noteworthy is that the courageous flyer stopped only twice to peck at fresh water ponds to replenish lost fluids. While being honored by his nation's ally, the United States, Paul Phillecroix V cast his eyes upon, as he put it, "The most beautiful bird I have ever seen." That beautiful bird was Piette Delacroix who had also recently been honored upon the same Capitol steps for her wartime bravery. A small wedding was quickly arranged where several diplomats and dignitaries gathered to share the couple's vows.

At the end of a brief honeymoon along the cool waters of Niagara Falls, the newlyweds returned to France and settled on a prestigious nesting place atop the l'Arc de Triomphe overlooking the Champs-Élysées within the City of Lights. After many years of attempting to conceive and carry on the Phillecroix name, the pair of lovebirds finally laid an egg filled with promise. They hoped and prayed that this egg would be the answer to their prayers. Piette knew that her body could not bear another hatch and that both she and Paul Phillecroix V could not bear another loss. Their last, a male, died in his shell just like the three before him, which brought the decorated war hero to his knees. Even before this yet to be hatched squab saw the light of day, there were expectations to uphold.

With a possible heir to the Phillecroix name just moments away, the entire flock was counting the minutes on the rooftop nest in hopes of a successful and healthy hatch. They had been through this before and those that didn't judge waited in hope and those that judge tapped their feet to match their impatience.

Chapter 1

"WHAT IS GOING ON IN THERE? The mystery should have been cracked by now."

Stephan Cambier, an aged pigeon of undetermined years and his wife of just as many, peered through the nest trying to get a glimpse of what progress if any had been made on the soon-to-be new member of the flock. Stephan had always thought of himself as a bird with a penchant for the comical but unfortunately he was the only one who thought so. After attaching one of his semi-quick retorts to the end of someone else's sentence he would teeter with glee, slap his unassuming wife Paulette with one of his wilted wings and say, "Plopped another good one didn't I Mother?" To which Paulette would always counter, "Oui Father, you plopped another one alright; too bad that it always plops on someone other than yourself," which inevitably received the laugh that her rotund husband desperately had hoped for.

"Would you two please put the pipe down!" What Stephan Cambier lacked in humility Madame Bertin surely made up for with her innocent and awkward humor. A dotty dove that migrated from the Highlands madame survived the loss of her husband, children and her right leg when they were sucked into the center of a ferocious cumulus cloud that seared them with lightning. Madame's nerves were shot through and through and the poor thing latched onto the first flock that flew by as she stood in the moor of her pain on the steps of the Paris Opera. Due to the shock of it all madame could not place the words of a sentence in the correct order and would spin and turn puns, lyrics and phrases inside out and on top of each other.

"Madame!" Paulette Cambier exclaimed, "I believe that you meant to say, 'pipe down' not, 'Put your pipe down.'"

"I meant what that I could have said and that was said was meant to be said she said of course."

Never missing an opportunity to stick his nose further into where it didn't belong, Stephan Cambier bellowed with the brusqueness of a circus hawker, "Madame always says what she means even though she has no idea what it is she means to say."

"I have my eyes on you Monsieur and if you should ever stop funning an opportunity on me at your expense I shall find it necessary to pack my valise and ship it to the local authorities."

"Paul?" whispered Stephan. "How much longer? My feet are killing me."

Paul Phillecroix' face didn't show the glory and pain of the hardened war veteran that he was. He'd fly a thousand miles for a friend in need and give you his last scrap of food if asked. Don't think for a minute this meant that you could take advantage of him. He could spot a liar at three hundred meters on a cloudy day and hear a thief at twice that distance. Five times decorated for heroics and bravery, he earned the right to all the respect and accolades that to this day are heaped upon him. He never sought nor needed them to define who or what he was. More than once he has been called upon by the Military and *The Council of the High Order of The Flock* to sit in a seat of authority and power. But Paul Phillecroix V was more comfortable with being in the center of the flock, and was referred to and known as, l'Eminence Grise, perhaps a more appropriate and accurate descriptor.

One would quite expect him to be hard-boiled but Paul Phillecroix never complained. It was his pleasure and duty to serve others and he had fully intended on passing these morals and ethics onto his children. Coupled with prudence and his famous family name and avian history, the world revered him and sought his council on a wide range of topics. He cut a strong and powerful figure and his sinew was elastic and surprisingly strong for his age. Walking in the park or down an avenue, the few that didn't recognize him yielded him a wide swath of ground, as his physique could be quite intimidating. But just underneath his tough exterior a smile glowed and once he trusted you it would jump and spring wide across his face. That smile could charm and molt the feathers off females half his age; united with his sense of humor, wit and knowledge of matters significant, dignitaries curled their feathers on his every word while women of the local salons swooned and cooed at every cock of his head. His wife knew that Messieurs et Mesdames alike would pluck the distal feathers from their roots for a chance to twist a delicious tryst with her husband. Paul was not ignorant to their advances however; he parlayed his experience, reputation, good looks and name into nothing more than harmless dalliances all to the appreciation and endless chuckling of his wife.

So, it was with a lifetime of miles flown and pounds of pride that the soon-to-be proud papa pigeon, Paul Phillecroix V, pushed his beak tenderly against the casing of his unborn squab and said, "The shell looks good. Good color, good feel, good texture. He's just about done."

"Or, *she's* just about done," Piette Phillecroix quickly corrected her husband as she stepped in front of him and gently sat down on her egg to keep it warm.

Unlike the smile that lay just under the skin of her husband, Piette Delacroix-Phillecroix displayed hers brightly in both eyes.

During the War Piette quietly left her parent's nest to

join the Resistance and supplied much needed services to her beloved country. She was twice decorated for her heroics and bravery and carries a small piece of shrapnel that tried to bring her down over enemy lines. Not only did she continue to fly like a speedy arrow with the metal lodged in her belly, she delivered her message and flew through a barrage of enemy fire on her return trip.

Like many of the ladies of her generation, she grew up with a lot less than those of the current one and never wasted a shred of anything. Her day wasn't over until the job, task, deed, or chore was completed. And like her husband, she'd sooner pluck a feather out of the center of her head to help someone less fortunate than do anything more than what was necessary for herself.

Piette came from a long lineage of highly intelligent birds and could easily out finesse her enemies with brain power and the poignancy and accuracy of her well-pointed words. Her linguistic skills were more powerful than most male birds could muster with all their strong-winged tactics combined. She learned during the war years to completely and totally shut out any and all distractions in order to focus on what was in front of her. This quality of discipline is what so many experience when they are in her company and seek for themselves, as she intensely listens to not only the words spoken but to the silence that lays between them.

Here amongst the chattering of the flock, she's going to need all the focus and attentiveness she can muster. The War thank God, is long gone and the birthing of this offspring carries far more weight and importance than the carrying of any message ever did or possibly will. This birth, to be sure, is probably the greatest responsibility that Piette Delacroix-Phillecroix has ever had. The vibrations that pulsate beneath her are a clear indication that a debut is about to take place.

Monsieur Cambier, impatient as a French poodle poked his nose into the Phillecroix nest and nearly impaled Piette with his crooked beak. "Attention! I do not have all day. Either bring it forth or I am going home."

"Silence!" Paul Phillecroix commanded. "We are trying to concentrate in here. You will certainly be one of the first to know as soon as he breaks through. It is the eighteenth and final day and the hatch will be upon us at any moment."

Along with madame Bertin and monsieur and madame Cambier doing their best to eye the first eye of the new born squab, madame Jacquet and her six boys, Jacques, Pierre, François, Guy, Pascal, and Nicolas alighted upon the Phillecroix nest assaulting it with a cacophony of adolescent unrest. Attempting to rein in her unruly boys Madame Jacquet was met with the same consistent and expected results each and every time: utter defiance.

"Guy, François come down from the top of that lightning rod this minute!" Do you hear me? I'm warning you. Do not make me fly up there."

If there is a quiet one in this bullish bunch of boys, it's Nicolas. As the youngest of the brood he isn't your typical spoiled last-born bird. He's been picked on more than most by not only his brothers, who have been known to dive-attack him mid-flight on family outings or tie his wings together behind his back while he sleeps, but by many of the mothers and fathers who live in the neighborhood as well. It's not just les enfants who can be cruel, petty and caustic. It's easy to understand the reasons children behave the way they do at times; their young brains forming and taking shape; chemicals spitting, spraying and firing in all directions. But adult birds of course, pardon themselves with collective bolstered pride and inappropriate behavior. They puff out their chests and rifle off an excuse to the likes of they've 'had a bad day' caused by the pressures and responsibilities of life, as if their children are somehow oblivious and impervious to their own stresses.

Once, while pecking at seeds along avenue Hoche with his brothers Pascal and Pierre, young Nicolas became the target of an overly anxious and obnoxious Jack Russell terrier. As the feisty canine chortled with his fangs bared and ears pointed, he took aim at his feathered target while two large male rock doves watched and laughed at poor Nicolas' predicament, snorting through their gaping beaks until Nicolas gathered the necessary thrust to take flight. He heard them in the distance bellowing to one another, "That Jacquet is one stu-*pet* bird." They tried successfully to connect Jacquet and stupid with a rhyme. "If the dogs don't get him the cats will."

"Boys!" Madame Jacquet once again called out. "If you don't come down from there this instant you will not be permitted to go play with your friends at the park this afternoon."

Monsieur Cambier had as much patience as a jackrabbit in a lettuce patch and tersely said to Madame Jacquet, "You have absolutely no control over those boys. You really must learn to show them who's the boss."

"Stephan!" snapped madame Cambier. "Mind your own business."

Madame Bertin, seemingly lost in the mounting melee of voices, provoked a losing conversation with herself. "Well, I should say so madame. Do not think for a moments notice that I would turn my head around to find you gone and if that were to be the example that you want to set for herself, well then so be it!" She countered herself with, "So is it my friend and so be it. But let us not forget who brought whom to this station in life. It was you that were left out in the cold to fend for myself, not I."

Huddled within its protected casing, the soon-to-be born was oblivious to the noise surrounding its temporary home. No one outside the shell could see it but perhaps Piette, if she paid proper attention, could feel a certain particular energy. And if that energy was or wasn't there during the other failed

Phillecroix hatchings, no one would know. One thing for certain, it's here now.

Across l'Arc de Triomphe down avenue Hoche behind a rooftop vent, a husbandless mother waits on her own squab to hatch. Natalie Caron never saw it coming: the disappearance of her beloved husband, the father of their soon-to-be child. One warm summer evening last year he went out for an after-dinner flight never to return. An empty nest was what Natalie awoke to every day, along with her broken heart. She spent the next six months huddled against the wall of her bare and crumbling nest refusing the food or water her neighbors had so desperately tried to get her to ingest. When she learned that she was holding the life of another inside her, she rose up from her disheveled state, pecked the nest clean and prepared for the new arrival. Life wasn't so simple for this single mother. Everywhere she went, disapproving eyes followed. She carried on daily with her head raised and met her responsibilities, ignoring the ignorance and indifference that attempted to destroy her. Her only offspring, a fatherless female, would in a few short months leave the confines of her overprotective mother in order to find herself in the freedom of the European skies. Natalie Caron will never forgive herself and she will rarely sleep, as worry and regret will be her constant companion.

"Paul?" Piette quietly called out.

"Yes, love?"

"Come, look. Here she comes."

"She? You mean here *he* comes."

"It's a girl Paul. I know that it is a girl."

"Piette, I am happy for a boy or girl as long as he can fly."

Piette batted away a tear from her eye and quietly prayed, "Please, please let this one stay with us a bit longer."

A tiny chirp pierced the rumpus in the air. It ascended up

and out of the nest into the Parisian sky and announced to the world, 'je suis ici!'

Madame Bertin stopped chattering to herself for a moment and the Jacquet boys came to an impasse in their roughhousing.

"Did you hear that," madame Bertin stated rather than asked.

Madame Cambier stopped eyeing her husband with contempt and turned her attention to the Phillecroix nest.

"Do you see that Piette?" Paul asked. "Look, he's making his way through."

Little by little the tiny squab pecked and pushed its way through the brittle shell.

"I do see Paul, I do and she is beautiful."

Unable to take any more suspense Stephan Cambier demanded, "For the love of gâteau what is going on in there?"

"I once came upon myself coming into the world just the same way as she is now," madame Bertin declared with a look of puzzlement.

"Here she comes Paul."

"Yes, Piette, he's coming through."

Jacques, Pierre, François, Guy, Pascal, and Nicolas pressed their faces to the outer layer of the nest intent on getting a view of the newborn.

"Stop touching me," François shouted as he shoved his brother Pascal with his tail feathers.

"I'm not touching you."

"Yes you are. Stop touching me!"

"Boys! Silence this instant!"

"Come, garcon, you can do it! Push. That's it son."

"She certainly is persistent, isn't she Paul?"

"He certainly is Piette, he certainly is."

The new Parisian had managed to make its way out of the shell far enough so that its head, chest and right wing hung over the toothed edge.

"Look Piette! He's on his way now! As long as the head and

the body are attached everything will be just fine."

"Help her the rest of the way Paul," Piette said.

"Non, ma femme. Let him come all the way on his own. Let him learn from the start or we'll be doing everything for him the rest of his life."

Piette stepped in close to her husband and whispered into his ear, "Écoute, there will be enough opportunities along her path to walk alone. Let's ease her first journey just a bit."

Decorated war veteran, heroic flyer, and man of great pride, Paul Phillecroix melted into a puddle of pigeon whenever he looked into his wife's eyes.

"D'accord, you are right Piette, you are right." Turning to their newborn their beaks dropped to the floor in amazement.

"Paul, look!"

"I see ma femme, I see, but I don't believe my eyes."

There on the nest floor a tiny, quivering pile of feathers lay panting with one wing folded under its petite body.

"Look closer Paul." He stepped in closer and was overcome with joy. "The streak! He has the streak Piette, he has the Phillecroix streak!"

"That he does, but look closer Paul." He stepped in as close as he could without crushing the little squab. "I don't believe it. I simply don't believe it. Il est la fille! He is a she! It's a girl! Mon Dieu, she broke through all on her own. I don't believe it. I cannot believe it! C'est parfait! There she is in all her Phillecroix pride and glory. My girl, my baby girl. I knew that he was going to be a girl, I just knew it!"

All of Paul Phillecroix' thoughts and feelings, everything he had known to be true and real and important, turned upside down. He laid a blanket of love with his eyes over his tender daughter. "Mon Dieu, she's so tiny. Smallest squab I have ever seen and still, she's so beautiful. Wait, what's this?" He looked at the newborn's feet and noticed that the hind toe on her left foot was abnormally short. "The one hind toe is stubbed. This is not a good omen Piette."

"It will grow along with the rest of her, you'll see," Piette said warmly. But c'est vrai, she is very tiny indeed."

Hiding behind their joy was the fear of losing this, their only child. They had come this far in the past. Neither of their hearts could withstand another loss.

"Do not worry Paul, she has the blue Phillecroix streak. She's a fine bird, a very fine bird."

"But will she be able to fend for herself? Will she be able carry on our...?"

"Paul, you're working yourself into a state. She's just a few minutes old. Give her time. We'll teach her all we know and she will grow to be who she is meant to be and that's all we can do and hope for. Now, let's bestow upon her a name that will tell the world who she is, so when she flies high or walks down a rue or avenue no one can say anything to her but, 'Bonjour mademoiselle Phillecroix'!"

Outside the nest the flock waited patiently for word until madame Bertin said assuredly, "She's here. I know that she's here. I can tell there is a newborn girl in there somewhere."

Nicolas knew too. He felt the coming of the squab and knew when it would arrive as surely as madame Bertin had. So did Natalie Caron.

"Mother," Nicolas called. "She's here. It's a girl just as madame Bertin said."

Paulette Cambier exclaimed, "Oh, my word a girl? Well, it's about time that we added another woman to the flock! I do say that it is high time for another revolution and that revolution is to be a feminine revolution and one day there will be…"

Stephan Cambier, growing more and more impatient with all the fuss over nothing but a pea sized squab said, "Paulette would you please be quiet and come along now? The show is over, there's nothing left to see here."

"Do be quiet yourself Stephan. We haven't seen the little

one yet. We can't just fly in and fly out without at least a glimpse and a wing to wing with the proud parents. Where is your sense of decency?"

"I left it amongst mes amis in the park whom you so rudely interrupted just as we were coming to a crucial point in our conversation."

Paulette Cambier could stand her own ground. She had never backed down from her husband as many French birds do and she wasn't about to start now.

"Monsieur, I assure you that the only thing that is or ever will be crucial in those so called 'conversations' with those friends of yours is who will be the first to steal some poor tourists' chips as they mull about the park. Go if you wish, but do not expect me to give you a warm greeting when you return home."

He gritted his beak, turned sharply from his wife and then shouted, "Phillecroix! Would you be so kind as to present the squab this instant so that we may go home sometime today!"

Inside the nest Piette and Paul Phillecroix groomed and prepared their child for the Paris pigeon world. When they finally presented her they were beaming with pride. A collective sigh from all but Stephan Cambier emanated from the flock.

"What are you going to call it Phillecroix?" Stephan Cambier asked without the slightest bit of interest. Before he could answer, Stephan Cambier sputtered another ill-timed utterance, "Mon Dieu, it's the tiniest bird I've ever seen."

"Stephan, you are much too rude. Please excuse my husband," madame Cambier said, as she stepped in front of him with outstretched wings.

Nicolas Jacquet maneuvered his way through the crowd gathered around the nest in order to get a closer look. Standing between madame Bertin and madame Cambier he pressed his beak to the crown of the newborn's head.

"She really is tiny," Nicolas said. "What's her name?"

"Yes Phillecroix, what's her name?" demanded Stephan

Cambier.

With a flourish of his tail feathers Paul Phillecroix V cocked his head slightly to the right with an air of aristocracy said, "We have not named her as of yet, monsieur Cambier but whatever we decide rest assured that it will befit her proud heritage."

Waddling his way closer, Stephan Cambier said matter-of-factly, "Well, whatever you call it, it can't be too long or too wide or too bold. The name needs to fit the body. She's scrawny Phillecroix so make sure to keep that in mind when you do finally name it."

Nicolas Jacquet looked at the little bird with quiet intensity and although only minutes old, the new squab locked eyes with his. Too bad, just moments out of the shell and already she's been labeled. Nicolas knows. He knows all too well. He knows what it's like to be thought of as 'less than'. He knows very well.

"Why not call her Pi?" Nicolas stated with an air of authority.

"Pi? Hum..." Paul Phillecroix took in the name and let it roll around on his tongue like a kernel of candy. "Pi, I like it. It's the root of Pipio who was the star bird of our family. "Pi...it has power and it sounds graceful. What do you think Piette?"

"Très, très bien Nicolas. It fits her perfectly."

Stephan Cambier inhaled and was about to cannon what would be another arrogant comment but thought otherwise as his wife cocked her head with a stern warning that he knew never to argue with.

"We may leave now Stephan," madame Cambier commanded. "Give Piette a peck on the cheek and a wing to wing with monsieur Phillecroix."

Stephan Cambier mumbled something under his breath as he walked over to the proud parents and gave his salutations.

"Au revoir monsieur Cambier, madame Cambier," Paul Phillecroix said as he waved his free left wing.

Piette addressed her friends and neighbors and bid them farewell. "Mesdames et Messieurs, thank you for stopping by.

Paul and I are quite grateful for your visit. We shall notify you by week's end of our little girl's first flight."

Monsieur Cambier was the first one to push off from the roof of l'Arc de Triomphe followed by madame Cambier and madame Bertin.

Madame Jacquet arranged her boys in chronological order as it was her compulsion to do in order not to lose them and because it was just about the only request that they ever obeyed.

"Jacques, Pierre, François, Guy, Pascal, Nicolas. Say goodbye to monsieur and madame Phillecroix."

The boys offered their goodbyes and then stumbled into their pre-flight pattern. Madame Jacquet looked once to the sky above and leaped from the ledge with Jacques, Pierre, François, Guy, and Pascal following her lead. Ten minutes later she realized that Nicolas wasn't in his usual place between Guy and Pascal and flew as fast as she could back to the Phillecroix'. When she touched down she found Nicolas still locked in his gaze with the newborn squab. What they were communicating to each other is unknown but by the look in their eyes it was something of significant importance.

Madame Jacquet gathered Nicolas and extended her apologies to the Phillecroix' and once again leaped from the roof insuring that her youngest was in tow.

Chapter 2

"AIGLE."

"Pardon Paul?"

"Que?"

"You said something."

"I said nothing Piette."

"Yes you did. You said, "Aigle.""

"Non, I did not love."

"My ears must need cleaning; I heard you say…"

"Aigle."

They turned and faced their daughter who was nestled into a warm corner of the family home. "Non, she couldn't have?" Paul wondered.

Piette walked over to her newly hatched chick. "Mon cher, did you say something?"

"Piette, she cannot possibly be talking. She's too young. Talking will not begin for at least another five or six days."

"Aigle," Pi chirped.

"Mon deiu! She speaks. It is a miracle. Tres, tres parfait! She's a Phillecroix!"

Paul Phillecroix rushed to his daughter. "She said "Aigle"! She knows her great birds! I'll bet she will know her stars in no time at all."

"Etoile."

"Did you hear that Piette? She said, "Etoile.""

"Deneb."

"Mon dieu! This is too much, much too much! How does she know all this? How could she possibly know Deneb? How does she know this Piette?"

"Because she's *your* daughter Paul."

"Oui, she is, she is indeed."

Pi was counting stars and learning their Greek and Latin names long before her peers. It came easily and naturally something that normally would have taken years of schooling by her parents and the elders of the flock. Although they were extremely proud Piette and Paul knew that on its own all the intelligence in the universe would not guarantee survival. Pi's continued existence would be linked intrinsically to her ability to defend and fend for herself by finding food, water, and shelter. There's no more deadly predator than that of life itself and all its unforeseen dangers. A bird without wings is a dead bird. Flightless, one can walk or run only so far so fast before becoming entrapped in the jaws of an enemy. But with a few flaps of the wings Pi could carry herself to safety in a matter of seconds. Wings create distance between life and death. The decision was made: Saturday next, Pi's wings would be tested for the very first time.

The sun rose slowly and steadily Saturday tucking the night into its resting place. Swallows living in the tall maple and sycamore trees encircling l'Arc de Triomphe began their day as they have for thousands of years by whistling lyrical songs.

The sun poured warm rays into the Phillecroix home waking first Pi, then Piette, and finally Paul who rose with excitement. Hopping over to Pi he said, "Today is going to be a day that you will remember for the rest of your life sweet fille." Pacing back and forth in the small nest like a general addressing his troops, he continued, "As you know you come from a very long line of brave and heroic message-carrying pigeons. You are a flying specialiste. Hold your head high, and look to the skies. Accept nothing less than your best, and then strive for more. You will be tested more harshly and more often than any other bird. You have a reputation to uphold." Puffing out his chest the blue streak running down it grew bigger and brighter. "Yes, my sweet, beautiful, little bird, today you will carry on the family tradition by taking the first of many flights. Bon chance, good luck!"

After breakfast with knots in her stomach Pi stepped to the edge of the family nest and looked down at the screeching machines rotating around l'Arc de Triomphe. Her face went flush, the ground below waved and rolled like the sea and her eyes fluttered as dizziness filled her little head. Teetering back and forth on the ledge inches from plummeting from the stone precipice, Paul Phillecroix yelled, "Don't move!" In an instant he grabbed her tail feathers and pulled her to safety. Her eyes turned muddy gray as she squeaked out, "Mère, père, I'm sorry."

"It's okay, Pi. We will not let you fall. We all started out the same way. Just trust yourself, you'll be fine."

She took a deep breath and once again hopped up onto the ledge. Piette and Paul Phillecroix shared a worried glance as Pi carefully peered over the ledge. Her instincts told her to leap but something else pulled at her feet commanding her to stay.

"Mère, père, I'd like to attempt this from the ground please."

They looked at each other perplexed. "Every Phillecroix throughout history has learned to fly the same way, from the nest," exclaimed her father. "It is not proper to take your first flight from the ground and besides, it's easier to take-off from here where you can glide the winds."

Pi's stomach ached from the thought in her head. "Oui, père, I know what you are telling me is true but I…"

Piette tapped her husband with the tip of her wing. "Let

26

her go from the ground," she whispered.

"Impossible! Every Phillercoix throughout history has taken his or her maiden voyage from above and certainly not from the ground. What would the flock society think if they were to see us sending our daughter, our only daughter, off on her first flight from the cinders below? We would lose all respect and credibility and not only that, it would be an insult to all of her ancestors – your family and mine. Non! This will not do, this will not do at all." He turned his back, tucked his wings tightly together and stood in his convictions; his every word coursed and cut through Pi leaving her gasping and wheezing.

"Mon Dieu! She's not breathing!" Piette rushed to Pi and took her in her wings. "Look what you've done Paul Phillecroix. Is it not enough that we have brought this beautiful child into the world? Have we not waited so very long to have a healthy, bright and beautiful child? Should so much pressure be placed upon her so soon? Is it absolutely impératif that she fly from the roof?"

Paul Phillecroix was listening. He'd been told more than once to loosen himself from his firm, French Phillecroix pride. But even so to ask this of a man who holds so dearly to tradition is a difficult task.

Piette opened her wings and unveiled a teary-eyed and fearful daughter. "Look at your daughter Monsieur. Take a good look at the bright blue streak running down her breast. Look at the love and devotion in her eyes. Is this not enough for you to be proud of? If nothing else you could…"

"I am sorry père. I am so very sorry that I have disappointed you."

Paul Phillecroix cleared his throat and bowed his head. "This is not good, not good at all. Maybe it would be better if she did not fly at all. Taking off from the ground is not an option."

"Fine, Paul. I shall take her down myself and enjoy every step of that cold spiral staircase." Piette could hold her own when it came to facing off with her husband. He knew too, that she would have her way with or without him.

With a glance towards le Sacré-Coeur, Paul Phillecroix relented. "Fine. If you want to attempt flight from the ground, then down to the ground we shall go." He waddled off ahead with his shoulders hunched as he leapt over the roof's cornice and glided down to the base of the Arc.

"Ignore him. He just wants what's best for you. Come, we'll take the stairs." Piette and Pi hopped down the long metal staircase to the bottom of the stone structure. There they discovered Paul Phillecroix strutting about the charcoal-colored cinders to the beat of an old tapped military rhythm.

"Ah, finally. What took you two so long? Pi, come here and stand next to your père. "Watch me now. First, you must prepare yourself to push off the ground with both feet at the same time. Flap your wings several times like this." He stretched his wings and beat them repeatedly stirring up dust and cinders from the ground. "Keep flapping until you're airborne and once your weight has left your body then you'll know what it's like to be flying."

"But I'm not as big as you are père. What if I go up and can't come down?"

Paul thought to himself, *why would a pigeon, a Phillecroix pigeon no less, be asking such questions? It is our nature to fly. It is who we are.*

"You were built to fly. The Great Bird made you that way just like all the other pigeons. Come, try flapping your wings."

Piette offered encouragement with a nod of her head and added, "There's nothing to it and when you're in the air you'll be so happy, so free soaring above the treetops."

But again a low, thin voice called to Pi deep from within herself. She turned back to greet her parents gaze. "I'm not sure that I am ready to fly at all today."

"What?! You don't need to be ready," barked her father.

"Commence at once!"

Trembling slightly she obeyed her father by first lifting her left wing then her right. She tried flapping them together as Paul Phillecroix had instructed but something wasn't right. Her father noticed it first; her left wing was barely moving while the right was flapping normally. Nevertheless, he encouraged and expected her to continue.

"That's it Pi, you're doing it. That's right, keep flapping those wings, both at the same time now."

She stopped. She heard something speaking to her and again she didn't know what it was trying to say.

"You're doing fine sweetheart," Piette offered.

Concentrating with every ounce of energy she had, she lifted her wings from her little body and began flapping them in unison.

"Yes, that's it Pi, you're doing it," Paul Phillecroix boasted.

Her wings began to move together. The tips of the feathers extended allowing morning light to filter through, casting thin striped shadows. Gradually her skinny legs rose from the ground as she was taken into the freedom that she was promised.

Piette and Paul's hearts rose as Pi ascended into the open sky. They had waited countless years to pass on their skills, experience and family tradition and the moment was finally here. Their hopes and prayers had been answered. And just as quickly, they were dashed. Pi plummeted to the ground with a great thud.

Silence blanketed the Etoile. She lay stunned at the base of l'Arc de Triomphe inches from the eternal flame. Her left wing lay crumpled under her own weight, the right pointed skyward. Her left leg throbbed and the right was completely numb. With gravel stuck in her beak she managed to speak weakly through her dented pride, "I can't do it. I knew that I couldn't do it and shouldn't have tried."

Paul and Piette Phillecroix gently lifted Pi from the

chopped stones until she stood shakily on her now swollen legs. She shook the dirt from her feathers and turned away from her parents. A tear formed in her pumpkin colored eyes and it slowly ran down her beak.

"Mon chère," Piette said in an effort to comfort. "Everything will be alright. We'll try again tomorrow. You are a French Phillecroix, strong and brave."

Pi didn't feel very strong and was sure she would never be brave. Now she knew what the thin voice was trying to tell her—she was different, different from her parents, different from all the other pigeons. Different. Even so, her desire to desperately please forced her to give her parents hope. "Okay, I will try again tomorrow for you père and you too mère."

Surprisingly and uncharacteristically Paul Phillecroix said, "Climb onto your papa's back. We're going home. We'll try again tomorrow." She clung to his broad back and they slowly ascended the one hundred thirty-seven stairs back to the nest. Pi never looked down.

"Père, mère? How do pigeons know what direction to fly if they've never been to where they are going?"

Paul and Piette smiled at their daughter's innocence. "Because they do. It is inside all of us; we know where to go and so do you. You know the way Pi."

"But how does it work mère?"

"It just does. Some things, no matter how many times we questioned them, will not change. Go to sleep love, you will need your strength for tomorrow. Bonne nuit. Good night sweet little bird."

Paul and Piette walked out of the nest and onto the southeast corner of the roof. The lights of the city twinkled around them.

"She's very smart, Piette."

"Yes, she is. Very smart."

Paul Phillecroix turned his glance towards the Eiffel Tower. A flock of geese flew overhead honking as they ascended in formation, disappearing into the night sky.

"It never made sense to me why those geese fly back and forth every year. It seems like a lot of wasted energy."

Piette smiled, as she heard this pronouncement countless times. "Yes dear, it makes no sense at all."

They sat quietly for a long time after the geese flew into the distance until Paul Phillecroix broke the silence. "You know as well as I do Piette that it takes a lot more than intelligence to survive. If she can't fly odds are against her…" He trailed off not wanting to press his thoughts into words. Piette rose slowly and took his wing in hers then whispered, "She is a Phillecroix and she has everything she needs not only to survive in this world but to live a long, useful and happy life. Whatever else she may need you and I will provide her in abundance. Let's go to bed. Tomorrow will be here soon enough."

Paul Phillecroix took a deep breath, stood, and as he turned away from the City of Lights, a shooting star soared across the northern sky leaving a trail of silver glitter in its wake.

The night was slow in turning and Paul and Piette Phillecroix awoke well before daylight. Paul had tossed and turned all night, waking Piette in his uneasiness. Unlike the day before, the entire family winded their way down the metal staircase and Pi prayed with each step she took until she reached the exit. Under a clear blue open sky they walked, first Paul Phillecroix, then Piette, and finally Pi to the center of the place de l'Étoile. Piette and Paul Phillecroix gave Pi ample time to prepare; too much time if you had asked Paul Phillecroix.

Pi puffed her chest and stretched her wings outward in preparation and then retracted them again. Her nervous parents watched and waited patiently until she was ready. She practiced again by puffing out her chest, stretching her wings and then began to flap first her left wing then her right. The left continued to move up and down in a strong, rhythmic motion, while the right struggled to keep up with that of its partner.

"Look Paul," shouted Piette. "She's doing it!"

Resolve shone on Pi's face as she flapped harder and harder in attempts to raise herself from the ground. Her left wing continued to move with precision while the right fluttered out of time. For a moment one foot would leave the ground and then touch down and then the other would lift slowly and then it too would come to rest. After using every ounce of energy she was able to summon, she stopped and stood exhausted, her chest heaved from the effort. Worn and shuddering with shame, she turned to face the rising sun. "I can't fly mère. I'm sorry père. I will not be able to carry on the family tradition." The statement buckled Paul Phillecroix' knees. Both he and Pi could hardly stand with the weight of their sadness. Pi's scrawny, little legs quivered under their burden. "What's wrong with me?"

Mother and father stood helplessly. "Do something Paul," Piette encouraged.

"Moi?! What can I do ma femme?"

"Talk to her."

For the first time in his life, Paul Phillecroix stood frozen in thought without anything to say. Piette nudged him forward with the tip of her beak and slowly he put one foot in front of the other and walked to his daughter. His head bobbed in a rhythm slightly out of time from that of his pink colored feet.

Pi couldn't face him. Not now. Not with her eyes filled with tears and her feathers creased and crumpled.

He stepped in close to his daughter, close enough so that their tail feathers brushed. He heard her sniffling back tears and gently called her name.

"Oui, père?"

"Hmm...everything will be okay...did you know that your great, great, great, great Grandfather, Pierre Phillecroix, flew only several meters on his first attempt?"

She turned her head slightly over her body to see her father's face. "But he flew père, he flew. I can't. I'll never fly père, never."

Paul Phillecroix' heart was breaking, and as he searched for something to say a speck of silver floated down onto Pi's back.

"Pi, I want you to know that your mère and I love you." Piette gave her husband a stern look. "What I mean to say is that we will love you whether you fly or not."

"What good is a pigeon that can't fly père? I'll have to stay in the nest forever never making friends, not going anywhere or doing anything."

"Sweet little bird…"

"I heard you and mère talking and I know what you're thinking and I won't let you worry about me. I know that you wanted a boy and I know that you'll never be satisfied with a flightless daughter. I can't live like this père, I don't want too. I can't, I won't."

Paul Phillecroix looked to Piette for help. Standing in the silence between husband and daughter, Piette considered her youth and her mother who had passed many years ago. Paulette would groom Piette in the afternoon sun and tell her stories of the Great Bird and many of life's valuable lessons. Now she looked to her once more. *Dear mother, please help me to find the right words to comfort my beautiful child.*

"Mère?"

"Oui?" Several thin feathers atop the crown of her head waved in the Paris breeze. She looked directly at Piette and stated, "No matter what you or père do or say, I will not be a flyer. Ever."

A cold chill ran through Paul Phillecroix' body. He looked to Piette who peered into his hazelnut colored eyes seeing his disappointment. She stood directly in front of Pi and firmly said, "Pi, I want you to listen to me carefully." Pi lifted her head and greeted her mother's gaze.

"Many years ago your father and I were invited to join the annual Phillecroix cousins' club where they were having their first cross-Channel relay race. Your father was so excited. He was strong, fast and eager to show everyone his talents. Each family member was to choose whom he or she wanted as their relay partner and I assumed that your père would ask his cousin Michel because he had flown the Channel many times. But your père surprised everyone by saying that he wanted *me* as his partner."

"What happened mère, did you win the race?"

"I started ahead of your père because he could easily have finished the crossing on his own. It was a clear day with deep blue skies, but the winds were strong and pushed back with tremendous force. I had barely left the cliffs of Normandy when my wings felt as if they weighed fifty kilos. I pumped them up and down trying to cut through the powerful gusts but halfway through the race I started suffering terribly and headed straight into the cold waters of the Channel. Just as I was about to crash, something swooped down from out of nowhere, grabbed me, and pulled me to safety."

"What was it mère?"

"It was your father, of course. He saved my life, again. But the story doesn't end there. He wanted to take me back to the safety of the cliffs, but I told him that I would be fine and that he should continue on without me. But your father wouldn't hear any of it. He secured me within his claws and carried me the entire way! We finished the race and the following morning we flew back to Normandy."

"Did you and père win the race?"

"No. What's more important was the fact that we finished. Your father kept flying with every ounce of strength and determination he could muster. He easily could have left me there or taken me back but he continued on. That same strength and determination he used to go on with the race, carrying extra weight and finishing, is also within you. Every bird has it; it's just a matter of tapping into it. Once you discover it you will see that it will carry you through anything, even the most difficult of times. The first step is to believe. Believe in yourself. Believe that the Great Bird created you just as you should be, perfect yet with so much life and learning ahead of you. All you have to do is be the best Pi Phillecroix that you can be and the rest will take care of itself. Your father and I will not love and care for you any less if you cannot fly. What is important to us is that you live your life with courage and purpose."

Pi listened to her mother's words and desperately wanted to believe but what if she didn't have the same strength and courage that her father had and what if she too became cramped and tired during her journey with no one to rescue her? What if?

"But I'm different from the other pigeons now mère. All the strength and determination in France will not get me off the ground and into the air."

"We are all different in some way. All of the Jacquet boys are different from each other even know they are part of the same family. Nicolas is much different from his brothers don't you agree?" Pi shrugged her shoulders slightly.

"And how about madame and monsieur Cambier, they certainly are not very much alike are they? They are husband and wife yes but they are two separate and very different birds who came together in marriage."

"Yes mère, I understand. I just don't want to be so different that the other birds will put all their attention on what's different about me."

Paul Phillecroix interrupted, "It's not just your differences that distinguish who you are. It is what and how you conduct your life. The Great Bird has decided that this is your fortune and we shall abide by that decision. We are a family and we will face this together holding our heads and chests high for the world to see."

Pi walked to her father and buried her head in his strong, feathered chest. "Père, je vous aime tant."

Paul Phillecroix stretched out a wing and invited Piette to join their embrace. And as they stood there in the center of l'Arc de Triomphe, the center of the world, Paul Phillecroix raised his brow and looked to the heavens and silently asked, *Why? Why would you cast this fate upon my daughter? I have served you well throughout so many years. Have I ever wavered in my devotion to you and those in need? Have I not answered your every call?*

The wind whipped leaves around the Phillecroix' legs and the sun stole behind a slow moving cloud. Paul Phillecroix was a patient man and had waited many years for the birth of his first child. Wasn't he deserving of a sprinkling of impatience?

Well? Answer me! He waited for a reply that he knew wasn't coming and then guided his family back to their rooftop home.

So it was to be that Pi Phillecroix, daughter of Piette and Paul Phillecroix V, descendant of Pierre and Pipio Phillecroix, a Blue Streak bloodline of the most famous, heroic and decorated pigeon family in the entire world, was not to fly.

Chapter 3

"WHAT DO YOU CALL a bird that can't fly? Dead."

"Pi, Pi she can't fly, I've never seen her in the sky."

"Phillecroix, Phillecroix have you seen a flying Phillecroix? Not me, I can't see her anywhere in the sky. Ha, ha, ha!"

The strength and determination that Piette insisted Pi had within her was often tested. The teasing and harassment from the neighborhood pigeons was constant and relentless. They'd fly by the family nest in pairs and taunt her endlessly then trail off leaving their droppings, laughing as they ascended into the Parisian sky.

The girls were worse than the boys. Acerbic and hostile for no apparent reason, they tortured the poor flightless bird reducing her to tears. One in particular, a nearly all white dove made it her personal mission to make Pi's life as unbearable as possible. She would hover high above the Phillecroix nest, wait for Pi to be alone and then speed towards her target. Launching her claws inches from the unsuspecting Pi she would then tear feather and scalp leaving her slashed, bloodied and bruised.

No one knew who this upstart was or where she came from. Some say her name was Dominique but Pi labeled her Diable; she acted like a devil with nothing in her eyes but fire and rage. Why this bird so detested Pi was a mystery, but her treatment became so bad, that during a nine month period Pi refused to leave the nest even with her father's guarantee of protection. During that time her feathers prematurely molted and she lost a lot of weight leaving her parents searching for solutions.

Paul and Piette Phillecroix organized the flock and all agreed to patrol the skies for the troubled teen, but she was too fast and brazen to catch. She had a knack for slipping through the flock's radar as if she were invisible, attacking Pi right under their beaks. Some of the flock's members who had been through combat in the Nobel Wars proposed to bring in neighboring birds to drive the ne'er-do-well into the Seine and drown her at the river's unfathomable depths. But surprisingly, Pi urged against such a plan and spoke at the flock's council meeting urging them not to harm or use force against the troubled bird. Even though Pi's life was severely altered by this girl's ruthless assaults, she refused to match her behavior with more violence. "She'll eventually stop. I will not worsen the situation with more hostility." Even when the elders of the flock, including her father, protested and tried to persuade Pi otherwise, she stood firm in her convictions that the harassment would eventually end.

Pi's protestations won out but the attacks kept coming to the continued frustration and disappointment of family and flock. The frequency of Diable's strikes grew greater and greater until they became a daily occurrence. Pi was forced to stay indoors interminably and as the days passed and grew in number, so too did her depression. She refused all food and water and soon became weak and gravely ill. Sleep was her only respite from the endless gloom and despair. Her words slowly dried up until she stopped talking completely and a dark and heavy veil blanketed her being. The world went on just outside the nest but Pi refused to participate any longer. Thoughts turned to escape. She spent countless days searching for a painless remedy. She weighed them all. The pain had to stop. She looked to the roof's ledge and knew its distance to the ground. She found her solution. She hopped onto the cornice, spun her head in one complete revolution taking in the city that was never hers one last time. Montmartre, le Centre Pompadeau, la Tower de Eiffel, and le Parc Monceau whizzed past her eyes. She looked down and took a step closer to the edge of the cornice. The long toe of her left foot hung over the side. "Mon Dieu, forgive me. May you have better plans for me elsewhere." She shuffled closer to the edge balancing between life and death. Wondering if it was strength or cowardice that she needed to take the final step, she heard a voice. *Pi, abandon me not.* It sounded familiar, like the voice she heard when she attempted her first flight. She heeded its words and stepped safely off the ledge and pleaded, "Please help me. Please."

Years went by until the other pigeons tired of their teasing. No one knows what became of Diable. Her harassment stopped and was never heard from again. The male birds grew older and bored. More interested in looking for a spouse, they flew off to the suburbs leaving Pi to wonder what it would be like to soar above the City of Lights or float in a warm summer draft, carried in whatever direction the wind chose.

The Phillecroix family was aging. Pi would soon need to think about caring for herself. No one spoke about it but they all knew that the day would eventually come. Until then, the family took long walks along the many avenues and rues that stretched out from l'Arc de Triomphe like spokes on a bicycle wheel. Avenue Hoche with its treelined sidewalks provided crisp seedlings to peck at and avenue George V and its outdoor cafes where diners tossed crumbs of baguettes to a pigeon and her elderly mother and father. These experiences were dearly cherished and they provided ample time for talking and taking in a meal together. Paul and Piette Phillecroix were now comfortable using their legs more than their wings. No one gave them much trouble and although, most were caring and trustworthy, there were those that needed to be avoided. Safety in numbers is the unforgettable pigeon motto. Paul Phillecroix was gaining in years and had enough bravado to protect his loved ones and hold predators at bay but this too, would one day change.

Chapter 4

TEN YEARS TO THE DAY in which Pi attempted her first flight, Paul Phillecroix awoke in excruciating pain and cried out, "Mon dieu! I can't breathe. There is...such...tightness and pounding in my...chest... Piette, do something." He wheezed through the tiny openings at the top of his beak, the color of his eyes grew pale and his complexion turned ruddy.

"What should I do ma chérie?"

"The...remedy. Get the remedy...from the forest."

"Yes love, the remedy. Tell me exactly what I need to bring back."

Gasping with each word he slowly whispered the ingredients that have been in the family for centuries.

"Leaves from a juniper tree. Seeds from an elm...fruit from a ginkgo, and..."

"What Paul, what else?"

"A small crumb from a croissant."

"Don't move," Piette commanded. "Pi, come here and stay with your père until I return."

"What's wrong mère?"

"Your père is not well and I need to get to the forest as quickly as possible."

"But mère..."

41

"There is no time to explain Pi. Please, just do as I ask, and I'll be back as soon as I can."

Piette Phillecroix pushed off from the edge of the nest and flew towards the Bois de Boulogne. Pi turned back to her father, who, for the first time looked helpless.

Paul Phillecroix knew his days were numbered. He had few regrets. He had been a good son and brother, loyal to his wife and loving of his daughter. He contributed to flock and country and was always there to protect those he loved and cared about.

"Pi," he said softly, almost cooing. "I want you to always remember that you are special in many ways. There will never be another like you. Someday you may have a husband that will love and care for you. I want you to know that it is most important that your heart soars, that you dream above the clouds and that you accept yourself as you are. The love that your mother and I have for you is boundless. This will never change."

"Père?"

"Oui, my precious little bird?"

Pi nodded her head and gently said, "Nothing père, nothing at all."

Alighting in a small green next to Lac Inferiéur, Piette watched several flocks of multi-colored Rock pigeons feeding and sucking up lake water. Several of the birds closest to her were singing a cheerful song in an unfamiliar language.

Two male birds stepped out from one of the small flocks and together said, "Bom dia. Como vai?"

Piette stood staring trying to interpret their lyrical language.

"Pardon mademoiselle, we are still learning our French. Please excuse us for not speaking so well."

"Monsieur, I am sorry if I have disturbed you at feeding time."

One of the pigeons, a big male who had a plum colored sack

hanging under his beak, stepped closer to Piette. "Mademoiselle, the forest has food for all, we eat what we want when we want. We welcome you, as we do all friendly visitors."

"Merci. Where are you from?" Piette asked.

"We are from Brazil but we have been liberated in France and now we live here in the forest. Only here, do we feel accepted for who we are. Vive la France!" The others joined him shouting, "Vive la France! Vive la France!" "I am glad that you feel welcome here. Most but not all, are ill informed about Parisians. We are friendly, as you can attest."

The large pigeon's plum-colored sack hanging under his beak grew larger as he said, "Who are they, and where do we find them? I will teach them something." He jabbed the air with his right foot.

"There's no need for that. Pardon, I must be getting back to my family."

A short, skinny bird tipped his head forward and said with a sigh, "Ah, family. We had no family until we came here."

"Yes, I am very happy for you, but you see, I am here on urgent business. I need the ingredients for the Remedy. My husband is not well."

The other birds started chattering to each other creating a din that carried across the forest.

"Ah, the Remedy."

"See, they do use that here."

"I bet that it tastes better here than at home."

"Quiet!" commanded the plum-sacked bird. Turning to Piette he said, "Mademoiselle, we will help you gather these things you need for your husband."

Within minutes Piette, along with the flock, produced the juniper leaves, elm seeds, ginkgo fruit and a large croissant crumb.

"Merci beaucoup. My husband and I greatly appreciate your help and cannot thank you enough. Should you ever be in the vicinity of des Champs-Élysées please fly by our home atop l'Arc de Triomphe. You are always welcome."

"Desejo-lhe umas boas ferias."

"Boa viagem!"

The pigeons tipped their heads and sang to Piette as she flew home to her ailing Paul Phillecroix, their sweet song trailing behind her long after she had left the forest.

Once back at the nest, Piette delicately laid out the leaves, seeds and fruit. The mixture filled their home with a sweet and pungent fragrance.

"How are you feeling mon chérie?"

Paul Phillecroix didn't answer. The color around his eyes had turned dark like that of muddy rainwater sitting in a puddle. He fell in and out of consciousness. His feathers rose and fell slowly with the movements of his breath.

"Mère? Père is going to be alright isn't he?"

Piette considered her response carefully, "Pi, your père is very brave. He has always taken care of us, and now it's time for us to care for him. I will not lie to you. He is very sick, and it's important that we do everything we can for him."

"I will do whatever is required."

"Should these leaves and things not help him, I cannot say for sure what will happen. Come, help me prepare."

Mother and daughter used their beaks to shred the leaves of the juniper tree into narrow and equal rows, approximately five or six per leaf. The seeds from the elm were then mashed and the fruit from the ginkgo pecked to reach the nut inside, which was then diced by pecking and stomping with the nails of their feet. The croissant crumb was left as it was. Piette then fed Paul Phillecroix a piece of each in a particular order. First, the seed of the elm tree, then a diced piece of the ginkgo nut, a sliver from the juniper leaf, and lastly, a tiny crumb from the crumb of the croissant. This was repeated methodically until every last piece was gone. After finishing the last of the Remedy, Paul Phillecroix looked at Piette and Pi and said, "Merci. Now I will sleep until the sun wakes me. Bonsoir."

The sun rose without showing itself. The air was heavy with moisture and grafted pale light onto grey and white swaths that bordered the entire city. Tiny drops of moisture clung to every surface.

Piette had been awake for hours, waiting and hoping that the seeds and leaves had done their work.

When a sparrow cried out for its mother, Pi woke. She lifted her head from her back where she had nestled it the night before and peered through the nest. She turned back to look at her father and caught her mother's gaze. They stayed fixed for a brief moment where nothing and everything was said.

Piette rose and in doing so woke her husband. "How are you feeling mon chérie?"

Attempting to get to his feet, Paul Phillecroix pushed his weight upwards. His heart and head pounded. His lungs ached with the effort and his legs gave out and rendered him a weak and broken down pile of feathers.

"I can't get up Piette. I'm too weak. I am afraid the mélange did not work."

Pi saw the look in her mother's eyes. "Père, what can I do? Should I go back to the Bois de Boulogne and get more of the juniper and gingko leaves?"

"Non, there's no need. If the mixture did not work last night then it will not work today."

"We should try again père. More must be better than less, don't you think?"

Piette had to explain the inevitable. The leaves and seeds had just one chance to heal. There was nothing else to do. Paul Phillecroix was dying.

"Mère, père say something!"

Piette Phillecroix fidgeted inside her feathers. Her voice was thin and scratches etched themselves into her words like those from an old record playing on a Victrola.

"Without the love, care and protection that our parents gave to us and that we have given to you, we would have not survived very long. Our responsibility is to raise and care for you in the hope that you will go on to live a full and healthy life. One day Pi, you too may have the pleasure and delight in bringing a new life into this world. It has been said for many, many years, that for each young squab that is brought into this world, two adults begin preparations for another life, one completely and distinctly different from this one. The cycle continues on, around and around like the carousel in the park. It, too, goes around and around and as the horses age and wither, they too, are replaced."

"Mère, why can't the horses just be fixed and keep going around?"

"There is only so much that anyone can do. Pigeons, just like the horses on the carousel, have only a certain amount of time to spend here in this life. No pigeon can stay forever; even your père, who has lived such a full and vibrant life, will need to move onto the life after this one."

"Why mère, why does it have to be this way?"

Piette knew there was nothing she could say or do, but Pi demanded, "Mère, answer me. Pourquoi?"

The Phillecroix nest filled with silence. It lay in every crevice, in every nook and cranny. Silence so quiet that beneath it, another silence could be heard and felt. Everything in the universe stopped. Time, motion, existence; all energy fell into a funnel that twisted, spiraled and turned down and alighted directly on Pi. Her legs buckled under the tremendous weight. Shock, sadness and disbelief penetrated her little body. Numb, she was unable to move a single muscle. She felt a desperate urge to leave the nest and fly away as quickly as possible to abandon and shed the incredible weight that was crushing her. She began flapping her wings, slowly at first, then faster and faster until the dust and earth from the nest lifted into the air and formed a funnel, except this one faced upward towards the sky and the earth and dust from her efforts moved with great force and pieces of the nest walls pulled from the floor and were sucked into the funnel. Piette and Paul Phillecroix' feathers lifted straight up from the depths of their quills, and it was all Piette could do to keep her claws hooked into the nest's floor, as Pi's feet slowly ascended inch by inch into the air.

The silence changed. Pi plummeted to the nest floor. The stubbornness of reality refused to give way to her desire to fly. Next came the dust and earth. They sailed and settled back into their original places. Piette and Paul Phiilecroix' feathers arranged themselves as Piette loosened her grip. Pi lay in an uneven little ball of feathers and tired muscles. No one moved. No one said a word. A tear hurriedly formed in Pi's eye. It grew, took shape, gathered momentum and rolled down her face. Gravity took it down her neck and to the roundness of her breast until it dropped and splattered at her feet.

"Père, is it true? Where are you going? Are you leaving us? Père, is it true?"

The wind outside the nest stirred and chilly drafts slipped through the cracks whirling around Pi's feet, evaporating what was left of her splattered tear. Tiny pools formed in her eyes and her head filled with dizziness. The Phillecroix family home began to twist and gyrate as the pools in her eyes churned faster and faster. Her neck fell limp and then swung like a pendulum from left to right and back again until it slowed and came to a deliberate stop.

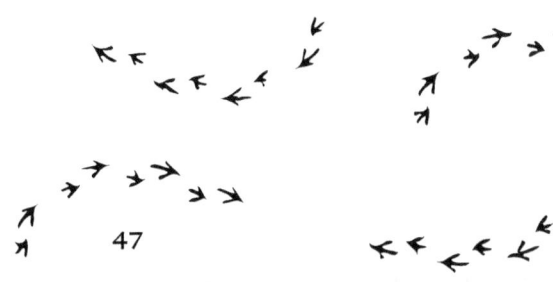

Chapter 5

THE ROTARY ENCOMPASSING THE des Champs-Elysées was quiet. Sunday's church bells were at least three hours away. A few white-tailed sparrows bathed themselves in the dried dirt at the base of the l'Arc de Triomphe. A young boy who wore khaki shorts walked along in the rare quietness with a honey-colored dog and alternated one foot on and off the curb. Tempting aromas from fresh-pressed coffee steamed from small bistros and the scent of delicious baked bread from basement ovens all over Paris floated through the air; it caressed noses, while Debussy's "La fille aux cheveux de lin" filled the air.

Pi was first to open her eyes. She rarely closed them during the night. Yesterday's events kept her awake for most of the night, and as she blinked small flecks of sleep from her eyes, the disbelief and uncertainty regarding her father jolted her fully awake. She looked over to her mother and asked, "Mère, are you awake?"

For the last eight hours Piette Phillecroix had kept vigil over her beloved Paul. She responded through a veil of grey light, "Oui, ma fille."

"Comment allez-vous?"

"Comme ci, comme ça. Et vous?"

"Bien.'"

Piette turned to face Pi, her eyes pale with weariness. "Are you hungry? Would you like me to get you something to eat?"

"Non merci, I'm fine."

Piette rose to her feet, her knees creaked from sitting on them all night. "I'll see if your father needs anything."

While Piette tended to Paul, Pi laid still in the warmth of the nest not wanting to move a muscle, not wanting to confirm what she already knew.

Piette called to Pi, "Come and say good morning to your père."

Paul Phillecroix lay at the feet of his daughter, weak and almost lifeless. "Père? Comment allez-vous?"

His eyes were ashen, his primary feathers dry and flaky. Yellow lesions the size of lentil beans had formed around the sides of his beak. He was having difficulty breathing but he managed to utter the words, "I love you," and then drifted off into a sickly sleep.

"Mère, is there anything that we can do?"

Piette shuffled her feet knowing of only one other source but considered it a fruitless option.

"What is it mère?"

"There is a doctor, a doctor that your père knew many years ago. They were very good friends during the War. He credited your père with saving his life on a mission from Paris to London. He considered him to be the smartest and bravest bird that he had ever known on and off the battlefield. Your père has said that he could heal the dying when nothing or no one else could."

"What's his name mère, where does he live?"

"Doctor Allbewell. Your père and he corresponded for many years and then lost touch. The last I had heard he was living somewhere on the southwest coast of the United Kingdom possibly near the Isle of Wight."

"We have to find him mère. We have to find him and bring him here."

"I cannot leave your père to go look for him. Besides, I would have no idea where to find him."

Pi perked her head and pointed her beak straight forward with determination and said, "I'll go mère. I'll find Doctor Allbewell and bring him here, and he'll help père."

Piette looked astonished. An image dashed across her mind of her only child drowning somewhere in the English Channel.

"Pi, I know how much you want to help, but it would be impossible for you to find the doctor and bring him here. It's too far and too dangerous."

"But what about what you told me? Remember, 'strength and determination…?'"

"Yes, I know…"

"That every bird has it and once you discover it, it will carry you through anything, even the most difficult of times?"

"Oui but …"

"And you said that the 'the first step is to believe. Believe in yourself'. You said those things mère."

Piette found herself entangled in her own words like a fisherman in his net.

"Pi, you cannot go, and that's final."

"What do you suggest mère? Who else is going to help us? Madame Lenoir who lives under l'Arc de Triomphe with her one good eye and molting feathers? Or maybe you think that monsieur Henri and his bastion brood of immature and stupid sons could find Doctor Allbewell. Or maybe…"

"Arrêt! Stop this instant Pi!"

Her mother's words shot out at her like a diving hawk stinging and piercing, putting a hold on her tongue. Mother and daughter stood quietly assessing their bruises, waiting for tenderness to act like a salve.

"Mère? Do you remember what père told me that first day when he tried to teach me to fly? He said that, "It's inside all of us, we know where to go and so do you," meaning me. He said, "You know the way Pi, you know the way." I will find the way mère."

Piette Phillecroix picked her head up and stood in awe of her child. *When did this happen?* She thought to herself. *When did she grow into this mature bird?* Piette stood on the parental precipice, a place where each and every parent eventually stumbles. A place where they teeter and try to stay balanced between trust and fear. Should they let their children learn and grow through life's experiences offering subtle guidance from time to time? Or direct, command, and protect them forever? Each decision has a choice and each choice a consequence. Piette tried to look past the present into the foreseeable future. Indeed, Pi had become an intelligent and mature adult and Piette knew that she had few if any other options left to help her ailing husband, but the possible dangers that lay ahead were so great and so many that she could not possibly let Pi go on such a tremendous journey. She stepped in closer and said, "Yes, it is inside you and you do know the way certainement, but I cannot let you go, it is impossible."

"Mère!" Pi protested. "I have to go. There is no other way, you said it yourself. You've tried everything. Doctor Allbewell is père's only hope."

"Non. Non, non, you cannot go. Who do you think you are mademoiselle? You will not leave this nest, I forbid it!"

An invisible volley shot through Pi's chest, batted around and went through her heart before it fizzled and dropped into the pit of her stomach taking her breath hostage. As soon as Piette had tossed her words, she tried in vain to lasso them and haul them back into place.

"Please try to understand love. I cannot lose both of you. We need to be here together."

"All this talk about courage and strength and conviction to rightness and the proud Phillecroix heritage - this means nothing now? How can you tell me all those things and then when it comes time to summon and use everything that you and père taught me, you tell me 'non'? Why mère, why?"

With equal strength, two invisible steel cables pulled Piette from the tips of each wing. Her body stiffened and her face contorted in pain. The cables twisted tighter and tighter commanding her to their opposite poles. She tried to break free but could not. The cables plied equal force and unable to bear anymore, Piette withered to her freedom and collapsed to the floor.

"Mère! Mère!"

"I'm alright. I'm just a bit light headed."

"Mère, désolé. I am very sorry. I'll stay mère; I'll stay here and be with you and père."

Piette spoke as if she were in a trance, "Pray for your père when you go to sleep tonight. Pray for your mère too. Pray for strength. Pray to the Great Bird for strength and guidance."

Pi would obey her mother as always. She would pray for her père and she would pray for herself and Piette, as instructed.

In the dead center of the night lies nothing and everything imagined. Stillness can become so loud. Peace is an unobtainable obsession. It takes just a split second for the darkness to take over the mind and create chaos.

Pi awoke in that dead center of the night with a pounding heart and ringing ears. She dreamt of her father being taken away without the chance to say goodbye. It was an awful death. She watched helplessly as he was torn apart, ravaged from sickness. In her dream he called and screamed, begging for her help. *All you have to do is wrap your wings around me, and all will be well once again.* But she couldn't. She was imprisoned by the night, dead weight bound to the nest floor. She tried kicking her feet but the night and her dream were too heavy. They smothered and pinned her down. She watched as her père gasped his last breath. His feathers fell out and all that was left was loose, withered skin, stiff claws and stringy legs.

She bolted upright, panting and heaving. "Mon Dieu, mon Dieu, mon Dieu!" Sobbing, crying from her insides out, she pleaded and begged to the Great Bird over and over and over for help. "Tell me! Tell me what to do...! I cannot simply stay here and watch him slowly die and do nothing. Please, please do something! Please...!"

She cried with fear and panic throughout the remainder of the night and floated in emptiness. There was nothing left to ask. It was eerily quiet. All she could hear was her heartbeat striking time in slow, rhythmic beats.

Natalie Caron walks. She walks the night into day and back again. Some say she never closes her eyes in fear of what might come around the corner or fall from the sky. So, she walks. She's evaded sleep for years. The purpose of her walking, no one knows. No one gets inside her thoughts. She shuttered that part of herself long ago.

Tonight is no different. She glides from her nest and alights on a soft patch of grass wedged between two poplar trees, which are themselves wedged between two tall paint-chipped buildings. Natalie only takes flight upon leaving and returning to her nest. The only other use of her wings comes when they're needed to avoid an oncoming motorcycle or imposing obstacle. Otherwise, she walks.

The tears in Pi's eyes began to dry. For a few moments she had no thoughts, only stillness until the stillness slipped away.

She looked skyward asking, "You are not going to answer me, are you? How would I even know if you did? And how would I know that what I heard was coming from you and not my own head? Why am I talking to myself? Pull yourself together mademoiselle, your family needs you." Her heart began to beat faster as her head stirred with excitement. "Attendez un minute. Think. Pensez, pensez, pensez. Think, think...I am...I am thinking...but nothing is coming to my petite tête... get doctor Allbewell here to help père. This is true...but how? How can I find him? Mère is right, it would be impossible to find him and who in the flock would be willing or even able to go and look for him?"

She mulled over her problem hour after hour. Finally, there was nothing left to do except discover what she unknowingly already decided.

She climbed out of the nest onto the roof. The night air was cool and breezeless. With a great push she leaped up onto the northward-facing cornice and stood on the exact spot where she attempted her first flight many years ago. It was quiet except for a few motorcars rounding their way around l'Arc de Triomphe. Nothing moved expect a small, lone figure walking, an elderly bird ambling in what seemed to be a trance. She walked up the rue, one foot in front of the other, head slightly bent towards the ground, eyes fixed somewhere in the future but nowhere in particular. A vacant look sat in the old bird's eyes.

"Why would a bird of her age be out so late? Poor soul. I wonder what happened to her. I wish I could fly to her, walk with her...Psst...psst. You-whoo, madame, up here. Are you okay?"

There was no response. The elderly pigeon kept to her drone of a walk. Pi stepped closer to the roof's edge. She teetered there keeping one claw planted in a small crag in the cement stones. "Bhhbbbbbbbbhp, Bhhbbbbbbbbhp, Bhhbbbbbbbbbbbhp!"

The old bird hesitated for a moment and then walked on.

"Psst. Madame? Bhhbbbbbbbbhp, Bhhbbbbbbbbbbhp!"

She stopped again and looked up towards Pi. A flicker of hope shone through the glaze in her eyes as she took in her image. The old bird began to gush and cry, "Odelette, is that you? Little Song? Your mère is here. I have waited for you. I knew that you would come back to me. Odelette, your mère is so happy to see you."

"Madame, my name is Pi Phillecroix. My mother and father are Piette and Paul Phillecroix."

"Odelette, why did you leave when you did? You left before I had the chance to be a mother to you, to nurse you, to instruct you, to feed you, to show you the world. Odelette, where have you been? I've looked everywhere. I have walked so many miles, traversed the City over and over in search of you and your father and now here you are all grown up! Come here, Odelette. Come down to your mère, we have so much to talk about Little Songbird."

"Madame, I am sorry but I am not Odelette. My name is Pi Phillecroix."

"Odelette, why tease me like you do? Come down here, s'il vous plaît."

O' this poor woman. "Madame, Je suis désolée, I am sorry, but it would be easier if you came up here, as I am unable to fly."

"As you wish my dear, as you wish."

Natalie Caron flew with surprisingly great speed and landed on the ridge of the stone roof. "Odelette, you are so *beautiful.* Très, très belle!"

"Madame, who is Odelette?"

"You are, my dear. My dear, sweet and beautiful daughter."

"Pardon madame, may I ask your name, s'il vous plaît?"

"My name, you do not know your own mother's name? I am your mère, madame Natalie Caron."

The name sounded familiar but she could not recall where or how she knew this bird. "Madame Caron, do you live in the neighborhood?"

"Yes, of course."

"May I be so bold to ask you a personal question?"

"I am your mère, there is nothing that I would keep from you."

Pi measured her question carefully; she could see that madame Caron was in a delicate state. "Madame Caron, may I ask your husband's name?"

Natalie Caron shivered as her eyes widened. The image of the vacant space where her husband used to sleep shot through the top of her head with the heat of a hot iron rod. She stiffened with the pain and stood on the tips of her claws. Her eyes rolled back in her head and her entire body began to vibrate and shake. Pi attempted to lead her off the edge of the roof using her left wing as a guide but she was stiff as a board and Pi could not move her.

"Madame, wake up! Wake up!" She shook as hard as she could until loose feathers slipped away and floated to L'Étoile below.

"Madame Caron, wake up, please wake up...please!" She slowly stopped convulsing and her eyes returned once again to their rightful place in the center of their sockets. Her body became limp and she collapsed into Pi's outstretched wings.

"Mon Dieu! Madame Caron...oh no...madame Caron...madame Caron..."

For all of Natalie Caron's travails she was finally at rest in the wings of someone whom she could trust. She gently opened her eyes to gaze upon Pi, who she thought she recognized.

"Forgive me mademoiselle. I have been wandering for so long, looking and searching."

"Madame Caron, I am so sorry if I have upset you. I shouldn't have asked you such personal questions. Please forgive me."

"I must have frightened you terribly. I have been living in a fog unable to see anything other than what I have lost many years ago. Pardonnez-moi, I don't even know your name mademoiselle."

"Je m'appelle, Pi Phillecroix."

"Phillecroix? Are you the daughter of Piette and Paul Phillecroix?"

"Oui madame."

"Why didn't you say so before? This is a great privilege my dear, a great privilege indeed."

"The privilege is all mine madame."

"Ah, you are very kind, just like your mère and père. Wonderful birds your parents, wonderful indeed."

"Merci."

"Do tell me, Pi. Why is it that you are not sleeping?"

Pi bowed her head.

"Now I see that it is I who has asked too personal a question."

"Madame Caron..."

"You can trust me my dear, as I have no one to tell."

"My père is very ill and unless I can find him help I am not sure how much longer he'll be with us."

Natalie Caron pinched her beak together and sighed through her nose causing the cere above her nostrils to turn light red.

"Pi, your père and mère are extremely fortunate to have you as a daughter. Is there anything that I can do to help?

"You are very kind to offer madame but there is nothing anyone can do except for finding Doctor Allbewell. He is an old friend of my père. I don't know how I am going to find him."

"If he is here in Paris then I can help you find him."

"That's the trouble. We only know that he maybe somewhere in England."

"Merde! Oh, I am sorry. Please, excuse my French."

Pi laughed and said, "Don't be embarrassed, I too have had a slip or two of the tongue lately."

"Your mère, Piette, is unwilling to leave your père's side I presume?"

"Yes, how did you know?"

"Some things will never change. She would not dare leave your father in fear of losing him. Although understandable, I do not agree with this practice."

"Madame Caron, please, I hope that you won't think that I am too rude to ask but would it be possible for you to try and find Doctor Allbewell?"

Natalie Caron thought for what seemed an eternity. She too, could not fly that distance. She was too old to make the journey. The losses she's endured; the burdens she's suffered.

"I would like to help you, I would. I know all too well what it is like to love and lose that love. I am truly sorry dear but I am not capable of taking on your request. I have not used my wings for long distance trips in many, many years. Is there no one else who can help?"

"Madame Caron, my père cannot wait any longer. He will surely die if he doesn't get the help he needs." Once again, Pi felt helpless but her helplessness soon gave way to determination. She raised her head and declared, "I will go myself! Oui, this is the only way. I will go and find Doctor Allbewell and bring him back to Paris, and he will make père well again. Bon, fini!"

Natalie Caron smiled at Pi's resolve. After all, she once had some too. She used it the day she decided to find her husband and sadly the day she started looking for what she refused to accept: her lifeless Odelette. Pi now remembered Odelette from the story that Piette had told her many years ago of how madame Caron lost her daughter. "Madame Caron, I know of Odelette. It must have been very painful. Knowing how much you must have loved her I can only imagine what it has been like for you all these years. I am the only child of my parents that survived. All the others passed just like your 'Little Song.'"

Tears flowed down Natalie's cheeks.

"Madame Caron, please help me to find Doctor Allbewell. Think of your Odelette. Think of my père and everyone he has helped over the years. Please madame Caron, please."

Pi was pulling at the already threadbare heartstrings hanging in Natalie's chest. "Pi, I know that you are unable to fly. Life can be so unfair and cruel. I want to help you, I do, but I cannot. I would be condemning you to an unimaginable fate and will not take that responsibility. I have lost my only child and I will not be responsible for the loss of someone else's."

She didn't lie very well. Her words didn't conceal her true feelings. Everyone knew that monsieur Caron abandoned her when she was pregnant and that everyday thereafter she cried herself to sleep.

Pi scrutinized her, carefully planning her next words. She loathed what she was about to say but time was quickly slipping away. "Madame Caron, if I was Odelette and was the only bird who could help you, wouldn't you let me go and get you that help?"

"Now just a minute mademoiselle. Don't think that you can hoodwink me by..."

"You would do anything to get your Odelette back would you not? My father and mother need me now like your Little Song needed you many years ago.

Natalie looked at Pi and saw so much of herself – resolve, sensitivity. Too much sensitivity, she thought to herself. *Others will perceive it as weakness. They will attack her and rob her. No, this one wouldn't survive walking three rues from home.*

"You couldn't possibly make it all the way to England and back on your own. Impossible! I am sorry Pi but there is nothing that I can do. Go home now and be with your family. That's where you should be." She turned her back hoping Pi would walk away without further protest.

"Madame Caron." I can't help but believe that you are not being completely truthful. I sensed it the minute that I told you of my situation. You are a fighter too. Please help me. Help me to save my beloved père. Please?"

Natalie's head ached from the internal battle she was waging against herself.

"Without flight it will take you so long and there will be so many obstacles along the way, some that I may not have come across even in my lifetime."

"And how long will it take madame for my father to die if he doesn't get help? I am willing to take any and all risks."

Natalie was losing the debate within. She searched herself one last time for permission to aid Pi in her journey and then said, "Quickly, there are many, many things that I need to tell you but there's just one thing that you must learn and commit to before we continue."

"Yes, anything, what is it?"

"You must never tell anyone that you come into contact with, where and why you are traveling. Do you understand?"

"Oui, I understand but why?"

"If anyone knows that your père is sick and might be flying off to another world, evil will sweep into your family's nest and commit horrible and horrendous atrocities. Would you want that to happen?"

"Non! Of course not."

"Then heed my advice and never tell anyone where and why you are traveling."

"D'accord."

"D'accord."

Natalie Caron instructed Pi for several hours on matters navigational: how to use the moon and stars as her compass; how to read storm clouds and test the winds for incoming hazards. She converted flight paths to those that Pi could follow from ground, deciphering signs, street names, bridges and buildings. She advised her on how and where to look for food and which rues and avenues to avoid and what and whom to trust and what to stay away from.

"Be careful of humans, Pi. When coming into contact with

them trust your instincts, and use your best judgment. Some will appear friendly and may even offer you a scrap of food or a place to lay your head. But be careful, for what they show on the outside may not be who or what they are on the inside.

"Your number one enemy next to the human is the rat. He will eat you in one whole bite, lick his lips and his stomach will still growl for more. They travel alone and in packs. Should you come across one spread your feathers, lift both your tail and your wings up high and drive your head forward like this."

She thrust her head straight at Pi, her sharp beak coming within an inch of her face propelling her backwards.

"Oh, I'm sorry my dear." She relaxed her stance and continued, "You'll need to be fierce and unwavering if you come across a predator as deadly as the rat."

Pi gathered herself and listened intently as Natalie continued with the lesson.

"Should you find yourself in an open field, keep your eyes out for hawks. They're fast fliers and they'll swoop down, pick you up with their razor sharp claws before you'll know what attacked you."

Imagining herself in the clutches of a strong and hungry hawk, Pi felt dizzy and her eyes fluttered for a moment.

"Are you alright?"

"Oui, I'm fine. S'il vous plaît, go on."

The lesson continued long into the night. Natalie Caron relayed everything that she could possibly think of that would help Pi on her journey. Over and over again she warned her about the dangers that lay in wait and even those that Natalie herself had only heard about. How could she even begin to instruct her about modes of transportation other than flight? Topographically speaking, most of everything Natalie had seen was from the air even though she hadn't taken to the skies of late.

"Pi, follow the Seine north through the City. Although the river bends and winds it will take you on a course due north and that is where you want to be. You will fly…" She immediately caught herself and continued. "As you travel north you will come upon Rouen and then Le Harve. You will then be at the northern edge of France where the land meets the great waters of la Manche, the English Channel. From there, the closest point to England and to Doctor Allbewell will be at Cherbourg. One of your greatest challenges will be getting across the Channel."

"Why is it called the English Channel if it is in France?"

"That's a lesson for another day, hopefully one that your père will tell you upon your return."

"Madame Caron, is there another way to keep my direction should I lose sight of the river?"

"Use the North Star as your guide."

"How will I know which star is the North Star?"

"It's in the northern portion of the sky dear and one of the brightest, as well. You'll know this star as every bird does; it's in your bones and it doesn't matter whether you can fly or not, you'll know this star when you see it. Besides, the current stellar configuration aligns with the precession of the equinoxes and France's position within the Earth's axis of rotation so that you will have clear sight of the North Star…Oh my, where did all that come from? All of my astronomical studies which I have long forgotten are barreling through my brain like a galactic bulge."

"How will I know for sure that I am looking north?"

Natalie paused and smiled and answered, "Because you will, because you will."

"I will follow your directions madame. I will find Doctor Allbewell and bring him here to Paris."

Natalie looked past Pi and questioned herself and her motives. *Me bénir. What have I done?*

As Paul Phillecroix fell in and out of consciousness, Pi and Natalie talked and planned throughout the night.

"Madame Caron, I want to say au revoir to père. If I should return too late I would never be able to forgive myself for not saying goodbye to him."

"That's not possible. If you go back to the nest now you may never leave. You must be fully prepared to accept whatever happens. You must go now. Go now before I change my mind."

Pi looked back toward the Phillecroix nest taking in every detail.

"Remember Pi, follow the river north. Stay on the grand avenues and rues, there will be less threat from predators."

"Oui madame, I will."

"And thank you Pi. Thank you very much."

"Madame, it's me who is so grateful. Grateful to you, as I will carry your Odelette in my heart with every step of my journey, and together we will reach England."

Blushing, she asked, "Would it be alright if I embraced you Pi?"

"Of course madame, I would like that very much."

Natalie Caron opened her wings wide and enveloped and held Pi tightly filling all the years of Odelette's empty embraces. When she finally released her and the warmth of Pi's body parted from her own, a small silver speck clung to the side of Pi's face.

"Oh dear, I've gotten feathers all over your face. Let me get that for you."

"Leave it there, madame. I want to take it with me all the way to Doctor Allbewell's and back." She took a step back onto the roof's platform. Pi thought to herself, *it is now or never*. She needed to gather up all her courage and find or borrow some more. She had never been outside alone, beyond the comfort and safety that the nest and her parents provided. "Au revoir madame. Merci once more for everything."

She turned, took a deep breath, puffed out her chest, extended her wings and looked down at the unmistakable blue streak running through her breast feathers. Slowly, she walked towards the stairs that led down to the base of l'Arc de Triomphe repeating, "I am a Phillecroix. I am a proud Phillecroix. I am brave and strong. I am not afraid." Reaching the top of the stairs she turned back to Natalie Caron and said, "Vive les Phillecroix! Vive la France!"

With each of the winding, spiraling metal stairs that she descended, Pi's feet rang out a petite chime that echoed to the family nest above. When she approached the final step she thought she heard, "Pi, I love you." She looked up into a swirl of darkness. "Is that you mère?" She waited a moment longer and then turned to face the large wooden door that separated her from the unknown. She bent her neck and squeezed through a crack under the door and spilled out into another world.

Chapter 6

Standing under the towering l'Arc de Triumphe with early morning sun pouring through its center, Pi is overshadowed by the immense structure. Small and uncertain she spins her head in every direction wondering which way to go. Avenue de la Grande Armée stretched out before her and the avenue des Champs-Élysées ran behind. Avenues Carnot, Mac Mahon, de Wagram, Hoche, de Friedland, Marceau, d'Iéna, Kléber, Victor Hugo and avenue Foch stretched to form the twelve points of a star. Une étoile, a star; the perfect place to start ones' journey, a guiding light attracting and then sending travelers to and from their destinations.

From the center of the place de Gaulle this bright star radiates and vibrates out through the surrounding avenues, boulevards and rues that crisscross and traverse the city from end to end.

"Which way should I turn?" Natalie's words came to her, "You know the way Pi you know the way." "I don't know the way Natalie, I truly don't."

She looked down at her feet and wondered just how far they could carry her. "One step at a time," she told herself. "One step at a time, but which way is north?"

She was already lost and hadn't gone very far: lost at her

birthplace. She would, if the universe would allow, look back at this moment and realize she had traveled very far: from the nest to the steps, from the end of those steps to the cobblestones under l'Arc de Triomphe. A great distance especially when you're alone.

She set herself straight for avenue de la grand Armée and walked past the Eternal Flame and over the bronze plaque with the inscription that reads:

ICI

REPOSE

UN SOLDAT

FRANCAIS

MORT

POUR LA`PATRIE

She turned left towards the tree-lined walk of avenue Foch paused, then turned right. "Which way, which way?" She traversed back through l'Arc de Triomphe trying to tap the inborn sense of direction Natalie had told her about. Coming to the mouth of avenue des Champs- Élysées she stopped and turned one last time to look at the home she was leaving behind. She scanned the walls until her eyes reached the sculpture, Le Départ des Volontaires de 1792 embedded into the white walls. She stood transfixed on the face of La Marseillaise with her chiseled features of determination and spirit. She turned, took another step and into her journey she went.

Attention! Get out of the way! Look out! Cars careened around the place de l'Étoile and screamed at Pi with their roaring engines and impatient drivers.

"Mon Dieu! How will I ever get across with all these machines?"

Woo-woo, Woo-woo, Woo-woo! Beep-beep, beep-beep.

Beeeeeeeeep!

She hopped back onto the sidewalk avoiding a screeching ambulance that rounded the circle with flashing lights and alarm wailing. "This never seemed so difficult when I walked with mère and père." She looked up to madame Caron for encouragement but she too was gone.

She turned her head left then right and left again but could see no end to the cars, motorcycles and bicycles speeding in her direction. "Go now!" she told herself as she looked once more to her left before sliding off from the curb, her body hugging the wall as her feet clung to the cobblestone street.

"Go Now!" She commanded herself. A small white car sped past her as she darted out from the curb heading towards avenue De Wagram. A swath of car-less street lay in front of her. She used every drop of fear that surged through her body to run towards the other side of the avenue. When she reached the middle, a giant truck came barreling towards her, its thunderous horn sending deadening sounds through her tiny ears. There was no time to turn back. The truck drew closer and closer and Pi's heart pounded faster and faster. Before she knew it, the truck was upon her and there was nothing she could do but say a quick prayer. A great rush of wind grabbed her beak and threw her head over heels and in an instant she was splayed on the avenue. She lay unconscious with her wings and legs spread in directions east and west and her back wedged in the cobblestones.

A great rumbling crept up the avenue vibrating the street's foundation. It grew louder and louder and when the gigantic mechanical monster entered the étoile it produced a ferocious roar. Down from its collective nerve center it bellowed awake the sleeping pigeon in its path. Pi lifted her head from the ground and saw tons of shining metal and glass atop huge, round rubber wheels barreling towards her. Drivers with intense and determined faces sat atop their machines calculating and maneuvering around the curve of the avenue. "Oh no, please." Just a tiny speck of nothingness in a bustling sea of impatient machinery, the trucks, buses, cars, scooters and bicycles were upon her in an instant. She flipped onto her belly and rolled to her left avoiding the burning wheels of an on coming car. Righting herself she tucked her wings close to her body making herself as slender as possible. Two delivery trucks, one with a pink fish painted on its side and the other with a faded decal of a bottle of orange juice competed for an opening lane. Bumper to bumper neither had any plans to relinquish their piece of the avenue and the right to claim first place. A green scooter with an enormous ball sitting on top wedged itself between the contending trucks; squeezing past both it came to within inches of running over Pi. *Beep-beep! Beep-beep!* With no time to react the horn-tooting scooter ran over the tip of her middle toe and sped off shouting, "Stupid bird!" The pain seared from her toe to her brain and back again. The city swirled, her eyes slid back into her head and everything went blank.

Chapter 7

Darkness dropped its heavy curtain. Crickets hidden in the grass and shrubbery scratched their legs and startled Pi awake. She opened her eyes not remembering where she was or what had happened hours ago. A passing dog barked and the heat from his breath jolted her to her feet.

Where am I?! She searched for her bearings and saw that she was on the other side of the place de l'Arc de Triomphe. *But how? I remember being in the center of the avenue, the pink fish, the green and white scooter and…Ouch!!* The pain from her toe told her the rest. She tended to her now swollen and brownish middle digit with her tongue, which brought a small bit of relief. *The scooter…but how did I get…? It doesn't matter…I need to keep moving.* She picked herself up and limped away dragging her sore toe with its claw scraping along the ground. Behind her stood the stalwart structure that cupped her ailing father and now fraught-with-worry mother.

"Come here fille," Paul Phillecroix called out with his ailing voice. I want to see your beautiful eyes."

The sickness had dug itself deep into the old bird's body. He mumbled Pi's name throughout the night as he writhed in pain. "Pi come and see your père…Where are you? Pi…?"

Piette hadn't slept much with Paul's tossing and turning. Once again she placed her head on his chest attempting to comfort and keep him warm. With each of his slow and labored breaths, her head raised and lowered like a buoy bobbing with a river's tide. Piette let out a small sigh. She knew sleep would not come her way anytime soon. She thought if she kept her eyes closed long enough, she could paint herself another reality, one where her handsome husband was walking beside her, his bright and bold eyes holding her with love.

She thought back to how he courted her and how he bowed his head over and over showing his respect and admiration. He fancied her and wasn't ashamed to show it. He danced an elegant ballet around and around puffing out his neck feathers with every deliberate step. And she followed his every move – keeping her feet planted, rotating her head like a lighthouse beam focused on an incoming ship. Seeing the memory again she gasped, "Mon Dieu! You beautiful, beautiful bird. My handsome husband, please walk with me again in the park, please…."

Piette looked at Paul's partly opened eyes. White and yellow pus seeped from the corners. She gathered herself and wiped away her tears, then called, "Pi, come here please. Pi, did you not hear your mother? Come here this instant."

Piette rose to see the void in the nest. Anxiety crept up her legs as her imagination took over. "Pi?" She called louder. "Oh, my sweet little bird…please, no…please…"

She rushed outside the nest and called for her again in vain. She looked in every corner and under every nook and then stepped up onto the cornice to confirm her worst fears. She peered over the roof's ledge to the hard ground. Her heart pounded in anticipation as she scanned the stones below.

Relief and regret exchanged places in her heart. "She's gone… Piiiiiiiiiiiiiiiiiiiiiiiiii! Piiiiiii!"

Piette's scream rang and caused tremors in each and every ear in the City. An aching parent's yell of panic and fear is like no other. It is instantly recognizable in its depth and sorrow. The sparrows, the Great Bird's largest troop of flying angels heard it first and began circling l'Arc de Triomphe. The starlings, chickadees and any and all remaining grey pigeons followed suit, creating deep rings a mile in circumference as they flew circles fifty meters above the Phillercoix' nest. Their density was so thick and color so dark against the Paris skyline that it looked like the middle of the night. Their flapping wings lifted Piette's scream through the circle of flyers and hurled her call up into the atmosphere in all directions for hundreds of miles.

The news was picked up fast and a large posse soon formed. At the north end of the city, one monsieur Gastineau arranged his flock and delivered orders.

"Mesdames et messieurs, attention s'il vous plaît! We are all here for one thing and that is to find mademoiselle Pi Phillecroix, and that is what we will do. Monsieur Thirrey, you and your boys scan the skies east to west from Arrondissement une aux cinq."

Similar planning began all over the City and it was agreed upon that the youngest Phillecroix would be located before day's end.

Shifting her weight to her undamaged foot, Pi trudged towards an alley in search of secure shelter. She came upon a rectangular opening bordered by a stonewall, itself bordered by guards of large sycamore trees. She looked for a crevice, a crag, something to act as a makeshift nest. Familiar sounds that she would have recognized at home, here seemed strange and frightening. The night whispered in her ear, *Go home. You don't belong here. Go home, now.*

"Who's there?" she called out into the darkness.

"Go home", the night whispered again.

She began to shake and tremble and called out again, "Who's there?"

"Mademoiselle," the night called back. "Why are you here in my park? Go away."

Pi turned her head in every direction but saw no one. "Where are you? Show your face."

There was no answer, only sounds of leaves blowing in the sycamores, along with a few sparrows dreaming. Branches started to rustle their leaves above Pi's head and she dashed to the west side of the park. The entire tree shook and swayed and stripped twigs and branches tumbled to the ground. Leaves and fruit followed as the tree continued to shake and sway like an awakened and agitated giant. Then it stopped. Pi stood perfectly still, she moved not a feather. Swallowing hard her throat clicked.

"It is awfully dark for a bird your size to be out here alone."

Pi turned on her heels but couldn't see who or what was speaking to her. "I'm not alone. My père will be here any moment now. He is very strong and will not be afraid of you."

A sudden gust of air stirred and picked up leaves that were scattered around the park's walkways. They stood and followed the wind's command and danced together as if they were holding hands, turning round and round in a circle, faster and faster until they came to rest in piles wedged in the four corners of the park's stone walls. An eerie silence fell. Pi turned her head backwards so that her feet faced one direction and her head the other.

"Hello?" she timidly called. "I have had enough of your games. I'm leaving now." She turned her head and when it was fully aligned with her feet she was met with a massive wall of burnt orange colored feathers. She followed the endless mounds of feathers up and up and up. There seemed to be no end as it grew higher and higher until finally she saw the beak of the bird that towered over her. It hung off its face like a jagged cliff. He was ten times Pi's size and must have weighed as much. She couldn't believe her eyes and was unable to look away from the feathered monster that towered over her.

Slowly and deliberately the gruesome bird tilted his head down until he was face-to-face with his uninvited guest. His head and face were misshapen. Where once a left eye was housed, now sat an empty, dark pit. Pi braced herself. She was certain that he was about to swallow her whole. Closing her eyes she thought to herself, *Great Bird, please don't let me die this way. Not here, not now.*

"Well? Please don't torture me. Tell me what brings you to my park."

Pi opened her eyes. "I am…"

"Cat got your tongue, mademoiselle?"

"I am on my…"

"Yes?"

"I live atop l' Arc de Triomphe, and I am on my way to see a family friend."

"You are, are you?"

"Yes, I am. Now please, let me pass or do what you are going to do to me. I have no time for word games."

The monstrous bird let out a laugh so loud and so wide that it blew the leaves from out of the wedged corners of the wall. "Well, well, well. You're a bold one!"

"I am not bold as I am anxious to see my friend."

"Where does your friend live?"

She remembered Natalie Caron's warnings. "Not far from here, a day or two's journey."

"A day or two?" He scratched his head with the tip of his

long extended wing. "Well, that would take you at least three hundred miles in any direction. That's quite a distance for a scrawny thing like you. Your wings don't look like they could carry you five miles, much less five-hundred."

Pi bristled from the accurate accusation. "Do not judge a bird by its feathers Monsieur."

"Yes, of course, mademoiselle. You are quite right. The father I never had once said, "You're not judged by what you look like, but by what you do to others.""

"And what is it that you plan to do to me?"

"Nothing mademoiselle, You are free to come and go as you like. This is a public park and you, I assume, are a member of the public."

"You said that this was your park."

"Well, indeed it is. I am considered the park's mayor and as mayor it is my duty to police the park and make sure that strangers like you are questioned and interrogated upon entering and leaving. This keeps the riff raff out and the residents safe."

Pi looked around the perimeter of the park and then scanned the trees. "Monsieur, I'm sure that you do your job well but I don't see anyone else in the park besides ourselves."

The big bird seemed to shrink a bit. He pursed his beak and tilted his head slightly before speaking. "You're a smart little one. You've got good eyes. You're keen too…okay, you may be right… nothing lives here but me." He bowed his head. "The rest flew off years ago."

"Why? What happened to them?"

"Because…because I forced them. I made them go and find somewhere else to live. I was tired of all of them doing nothing but doing everything for me – getting me breakfast, catering to my every request just because they were afraid of me. It became so boring. Oh, I can scare anything that stumbles into the park but nobody comes here any more. The word's been out for so long and everyone avoids me. What's the point of being so big when there's no one left to push around? It's no fun anymore, no fun at all and now I have no one to talk with and nothing to do."

"That seems a fair price to pay. All you've ever done is keep others away when what you really wanted was to have them near. You've accomplished what you always wanted and now you're alone and you blame all the creatures that you frightened off for your loneliness. That's very sad."

The big bird shrank further. His body fell like an elevator plummeting to the ground. He stopped at Pi's eye level, paused and then dropped further, as if the cornerstone of a building was plucked and the entire structured toppled. "What is happening to me?"

"You've shrunk."

"How can this be happening? A bird can't just..."

Pi tried hiding her amusement, "Maybe you've become so big with yourself and then with no one left to scare and bully you've come down to your appropriate size?"

"I don't wanna' be so small. I don't like it. I feel…"

"Afraid?"

"Yes, and I don't like it, I don't like it at all. It is not me. I'm better than this. I'm tougher and stronger. I can take down any bird! I will not be the same size as you. You can't even fly two days' worth and here I am the same size as you and feeling…I can't even say the word! This is not happening to me…non, non, non!"

"You only think that you're better than all the other birds. You misjudge others when you don't even know them. You don't know what their story is, what they may have gone through or where they came from or the heartaches that they've endured or the family and friends they may have lost. You're too busy thinking of yourself to be aware of anyone else."

Her truths struck the once big bird in the center of his chest. He considered pouncing on her but he just condensed

75

further and further until his beak lay flat on the ground between his tiny feet.

For once Pi was looking down on someone else. She felt powerful, confident, commanding. It was something she hadn't experienced before.

"Please have pity on me. I never meant to do or say the things I said or did...I'm bourgeois pretending to be someone that I'm not. Not that there is anything wrong with being a member of the bourgeois. Not at all, it's just that when you've been told your entire life by the birds who tell you these things - these birds who know everything, you start to believe them and they stick to you like feathers to tar and then they're hard to get out because they've stuck so deep."

"What things?"

"That you're no good, that...that..."

"Go on, I want to know."

"That you are..." He rolled his eyes up to look at Pi. "That you're not even noticed or recognized by these birds that told you these things."

"Monsieur, I think I understand."

"You do?"

"Oui."

"Bon. Then would you please be so kind as to explain it to me?"

"Non, there's no need to discuss it any further. Besides, I need to continue on my journey. I regret that I cannot stay any longer."

"But please, mademoiselle. Don't leave me now. We were just starting to become close friends. If you leave now I'll never know the answer to my question."

The situation was becoming quite hopeless. Pi had to move on. If she allowed it he could keep her there forever.

"Monsieur, bonne nuit. I am leaving now. Au revoir."

She walked quickly to the edge of the park without looking

back.

"Wait! What is your name?"

"Pi Phillecroix. And yours?"

"Trigg."

"Au revoir Trigg."

"Wait!" He shouted again, as Pi walked away. Is your père the Paul Phillecroix?"

She didn't answer him. The dejected bird's howls followed her into the night.

Darkness clamped down on the city. Moving about was strained and strenuous for anyone not experienced in nocturnal travel. Pi's eyesight was acute but was affected by her confidence and the knocking in her knees. She paused and searched for signs of wilted daylight between the trees and spotted a large flock of birds circling, looking for something. *They're probably just as hungry as I am.*

Chapter 8

Pi walked in a hazy fog all night until she arrived in an abandoned field of overgrown weeds and twisted trees that rambled through an abandoned and crumbled building near Marie Saint Ouen. A gash in a rusted drainpipe would provide a night of shelter. She hadn't had anything in her stomach since she left home. As she walked toward the east side of the field she noticed two young male pigeons shouting nonsensical things at each other. One of them noticed her and started whistling, "Hey there little lady. Got time for me?" She ignored him, kept her head down and picked up her pace.

"I said, *hey there!* Don't you hear good?"

"Better than you speak." She whispered under a breath.

"What did you say?"

"Nothing, nothing at all. I am minding my own business. I suggest you do the same."

"Too late for that isn't it?"

Dandre was a slender pigeon with short, cropped feathers atop his head and a long gash down his chest that ended at the middle of his belly. His feathers, muted and multi-colored, gave him the look of a court jester who hadn't changed his clothes in years. His voice, high-pitched and nasal, caused him to whistle his words through his nose. Mocking Pi he said, "Minding my own businesssss, she said. Did you hear her, Raoul?"

Raoul, quite unlike Dandre, was short, round and bore a permanent limp on his right leg, the product of a fight with a hawk that he never asked to be part of. His feathers were shinier and healthier than that of his friend's, and if you got to know him you might be surprised by the amount of street knowledge he had stored away in his short, fifteen years. His voice was a tenor and lent him more confidence and authority than he actually owned.

"Leave her alone. She's not bothering us."

"Who are you to tell me what to do?" Dandre scorned.

"I'm just saying, Dandre, that we have bigger birds to fry than her."

Dandre considered Raoul for a minute with one eye and then turned back to Pi. "Non. I think she's just the right size for frying."

"Pardon but there will be no frying of any sort where I am concerned," Pi boldly instructed. "Furthermore, I am too hungry and tired to converse with you two gentleman any further. Adieu."

She took a few steps forward and was met with one of Dandre's strong, stiff wings. "You're not going anywhere. And '*furthermore*', whatever that means, you now belong to us. Right Raoul?"

Raoul measured Dandre's icy face and as he had done countless times, pathetically capitulated. "Right Dandre. She's ours."

"Let's hang her."

"Come on Dandre, let's just go sit near the river."

"Don't you tell me what to do Raoul or I'll hang you both. If you ain't tough enough to hang her then go and play with some girls."

"I'm just saying…"

"*I'm just say, 'I'm just sayin…'* That all you say, is *'I'm just sayin.'"* "Toughin' up or get the hell out of here!"

"Okay, okay. I'll do it."

Dandre smiled sadistically. A lump bulged in Raoul's throat. He knew Dandre's capabilities and once Raoul decided to do what he knew he shouldn't do, his personality was hijacked and there was no turning back.

"Messieurs, if it's all the same to you, I prefer not to be hanged today."

"Did you hear that Dandre? She'd *prefer* not to be hanged today."

Dandre's face oozed evil. He loved seeing Raoul so easily persuaded to wickedness.

"So, what do you suggest we do with her Raoul?"

"I say we hang her from the tallest tree." He looked upwards. "Which, I believe we are standing under."

Dandre tilted his head. "Yes, I think you're right my smart friend. This tree will do just fine."

"Monsieur Dandre, monsieur Raoul," Pi pleaded. "I don't think that you want to do this. My père is Paul Phillecroix and…"

"Did you hear that Raoul? Her father is Paul Phillecroix. Yeah, and I'm a Bald Eagle."

Dandre and Raoul roared with laughter at Pi's seemingly ridiculous statement.

"It's true. He really is my père."

"Ha, ha, ha. Even if he was he's not here now!"

"Yeah, what's he gonna' do for you now?" mocked Raoul.

"Get her up the tree Raoul."

"Oui Monsieur."

"Please, I am on a very important mission. I must leave here instantly. I am sure that your day will be much enhanced without hanging me."

Dandre and Raoul carefully inspected Pi from head to claws. There was a brief pause where Pi thought she saw a speck of sympathy in Raoul's eyes.

"How high should I take her Dandre?"

"All the way." Raoul jumped and bit down hard on the back of Pi's neck paralyzing her.

"Good job Raoul. Now take her to the highest branch."

Raoul obediently obeyed and flew to the top of the tree with Pi drooping from his beak. She looked like a lifeless rag doll - her head slumped to her chest and her feet dangled in the morning breeze. Raoul alighted on the highest branch, transferred Pi to his claw and hung her upside down. Their combined weight caused the branch to sag and wave.

On an adjacent leafless branch, Dandre perched himself where he could orchestrate the proceedings. "Let her go. I want to see what she'll look like when she crashes from branch to branch. She'll get to the ground in a thousand pieces!"

"Ya', maybe she'll end up getting a sharp one right through the chest and her blood will spurt all over and then we'll leave her there until she rots."

Pi was filled with more fear than she'd ever imagined possible. The blood rushed to her head and her eyes felt as if they were about to pop out of her face.

"Look, look her eyes are coming out of her head," howled Dandre. "That's très cool. When they pop out we'll spit them at the old birds!"

A heavy wind blew across the treetops and Dandre and Raoul instinctively grabbed tightly to their branches. Pi tilted her head slightly and looked past her captors and saw a large, dark-colored, cross-shaped thing descending from the sky to the very tip of the tree. It pushed heavy drafts of air down causing the leaves and branches to bow and bend and the feathers of the three birds to wrap and cling to their bodies, trapping them making it impossible to move.

Raoul could barely open his beak to speak, and his words were split and broken from the powerful force pushing down on him. "Whaaa…isss…thaa…thing?"

The drafts of wind grew heavier and heavier until they finally slowed and the tree and all of its leaves and branches sprung back to their upward sloping shapes. Raoul and Dandre twitched and shook their feathers and stretched their wings. Blood dropped from their claws splattering Pi's face. Stunned and numbed with pain, she stared at the thing at the top of the tree attempting to bring it into focus. Its own eyes looked down as it lengthened its neck. Its head moved slowly down the tree towards Raoul and Dandre. Its neck unraveled and grew longer and moved liked a giant snake. When its head came to within a few feet of Raoul and Dandre they screamed in panic.

And then it was gone. But Dandre and Raul filled with panic begged, "Please don't eat us. Please!" Raoul shook in his orange feet and dug his claws further into Pi causing her to whither and shriek in pain. "Agghhhhhhhhhhhhhhhhhh!!"

Pi righted herself so that she was now on top of the branch and Dandre and Raoul were hanging underneath.

Dandre screamed in fear, "Whoa! Don't let go little girl, don't let go!"

Pi assumed a deep, firm and masculine voice, "What did this little bird do to deserve the hanging you have given her?"

"We were just having fun, just a little fun weren't we Raoul?"

"That's right, just a little fun."

With their eyes still shut and hanging precipitously from the branch, she then asked, "How much fun are you having now?" They muttered a few "none" and "sorry" followed by sobs.

"I will take from your silence that you are not enjoying yourselves very much?" Dandre and Raoul whimpered and nodded their heads. "I'm going to let go now."

"What!" Screamed Dandre. "If you let go, we'll fall."

"You can fly can't you?" Pi asked reveling in their predicament.

"Yes, but not upside down."

"You should have thought of that before you took advantage of one so much smaller than you."

"We meant no harm."

"It's a bit late for that, isn't?" Pi asked, still assuming a deep and powerful voice. "Now messieurs, you will loosen your grip and pull your claws away on the count of trois. Do you understand?"

"Oui Monsieur."

"Good. Un, deux, trois, allez!" Pi let go of her penetrating grip and Dandre and Raoul slowly began to lose their hold. They hollered out, "Non!" "Arrêt ! I'm sorry." In the blink of an eye, Dandre and Raoul dropped and within a few feet from the ground righted themselves and flew off with battered pride. As they did, Pi called out, "Messieurs commit to leaving in peace those that you would so quickly take advantage of."

A few of Raoul and Dandre's breast feathers that were stuck to the tree branch lost their hold and drifted away. Pi spent the better part of two hours maneuvering herself down the tree from one branch to another, hopping, sliding and jumping until she finally reached its base. She then proceeded to walk southeast across the field in hopes of finding the Seine.

Three brightly colored starlings sat in one tree in the middle of seven others in the center of a wedge in the middle of the place de la République.

One, a mostly purple-colored bird, sat between the two others. He barked more than chirped a strange call while the one to his left, a shiny green one, repeated every call and every word spoken within earshot. This was no small feat, for his hearing was incredibly sharp, which left his head in a constant buzz of words and sounds; his mouth and body in constant motion.

One of the other birds specked with grey, was more yellow than green and less shiny than her friends. She sat further apart from the others and said nothing and was content to straddle the branch as it bobbed and weaved with the wind.

The mostly purple-colored one turned to the shiny green bird and said, "I can't help it, I can't stop. I've tried. Oh, Lord I have tried. Oh, Lord I have tried. Think how it is for me. I hear everything three times! Once when you say it, then again when I repeat it and again when I repeat and again when I repeat it again. You see? You see? You see?" While repeating himself something caught his attention coming toward the wedge. "Look, look, look. Who's that, that, that…"

"Shut up! Please shut up!"

"Shut up, shut up, shut up. Try barking that barking bird."

The purple barking bird noticed Pi coming toward the wedge, "Look, look, look!"

"Now you're doing it, see, see, see?"

"Yes, I see."

"Yes, I see. Yes, I see. Yes, I see."

"No, I do see. Shut up!"

With the humiliation of Raoul and Dandre behind her, Pi had walked just a few blocks when she came upon the wedge of the place de la République.

The purple bird hopped off his perch and glided down to her. "And what brings us this great pleasure of your presence today?"

"I am just walking through the day, that is all."

"I am just walking through the day, just walking through the day, just walking through the day."

"Are you teasing me monsieur? Because I have had enough teasing and torment of late and I do not wish for more.

"Non, non, non! Pardon mademoiselle. I hear everything

three times! Once when you say it, then again when I repeat it and again when I repeat and again when I repeat it again. You see? You see? You see?"

"It must be very frustrating."

"It must be very frustrating. It must be very frustrating. It must be very frustrating."

The purple-colored barking bird barked with laughter and doubled over, holding his stomach in pain. The grey speckled bird turned her head away. She has seen and heard all this more times than she cared to remember. She thought to herself as she has for years, *If only I could leave these two I would.*

"Oh, I am sorry, mademoiselle. I truly and honestly and earnestly have no intentions of teasing. Where are you coming from mademoiselle?"

"I live here in the City as you do. My home is wherever I am."

"Very esoteric," the shiny green bird barked as he rolled his eyes. "That just means that you're homeless."

"Monsieur, I assure you that I have a home and a family and I need not discuss this with you any further." She started for the other side of the wedge. "I am just out for a walk. Can't one just walk and not be questioned?"

"Questioned, questioned, questioned." The purple colored repeating bird repeated with abandon. "Oh no, now you've done it! I'm upset and you know what happens when I'm upset."

"Monsieur, I am sorry if I…"

"Not you mademoiselle, him!" He pointed his head at the shiny bird. "He knows not to raise his voice, he knows how it makes me…I've told you Horace…I have told you time and time and time again!"

"I'm sorry Bertrand. I forgot." It was too late.

"I forgot. I forgot! I forgot! I forgot!! I forgot!!! I forgot!! I forgot!!!" His voice grew louder and louder and he could not break his repetition. "I forgot!!! I forgot!!!! I forgot!!!!!"

The grey speckled bird alighted next to Bertrand shaking him with her right wing. "Bertrand! Aret! Aret Bertrand!"

"Je ne veux pas mourir seul."

"Bertrand, you are not going to die alone." She had heard his insecure cries many times before and had grown weary of them a long time ago. "We're here with you if you die."

"Die, die, die!"

"S'il vous plaît arrêter." Pi pleaded. "Stop saying that!"

A thwack of thunder boomed across the City and shook the foundation for miles. Bertrand stopped repeating and looked up to the darkening sky. Horace and the grey speckled bird looked at each other and flew off leaving Pi and Bertrand alone on the wedge.

"Get out, get out, get out!" Bertrand commanded."

"Get out to where?" Pi asked. It's just a thunderstorm."

"Non, non, non! It's not just any thunderstorm; it's a Turpain storm! Get out, get out, get out!" Bertrand leapt into the air; the winds from the whirling storm flung him out over the Seine until the dark sky swallowed him. His warning echoed behind him.

"Turpain? What is a Turpain storm?" No sooner had she asked, the sun was stomped out by thick storm clouds. Drops of rain fell lightly at first then yielded to pelting hail. The balls of hail were large and round and stung through her feathers, driving her into the street's gutter. The hail and rain gathered into a rolling surge that upended Pi and sent her towards an awaiting sewer grate. On her back down the rue she went. She attempted over and over to right herself but the current was too strong against her tiny body. She could see the stream of water surge down into darkness in front of her.

"Aidez-moi, s'il vous plaît!" She screamed, as she poured down a storm drain along with discarded newspapers, frayed and hastily puffed cigarettes, partially eaten sandwiches, and an array of cans, bottles, and bottle caps. Tossed down to the bottom of a dark pool of filth she fought with wings, claws and feet to get back to the top of the pool. Once there, she gasped and wheezed through the unabated flow of water that poured through the sewer and crashed down upon her head.

"I can't…breathe…"

Fighting for every breath, she kept herself from being pulled back to the bottom of the muddy pool and managed to push herself to the safety of a stone overhang. Through the cascading waterfall she gulped as much air as she could and when her lungs were finally satiated, the precipice she clung to, collapsed. Plunged once again into the dark and infested water, she fought the force and current that outweighed her a million times to one. Carried off to a down chute that pitched her to an awaiting drain hole that dumped her to unknown depths, she fought with the current trying to keep her head above the surface. As she did, she caught glimpses of shadows and squeaks of sounds from bends, corners, junctions and intersections of the dark and murky subterranean passage.

Shrills of hidden and unseen voices shouted and pierced from every direction. Atop a small mound on the right side of a fork in the waterway, hot red eyes glared and glowed like precision laser beams. They burned their excitement and anticipation deep into Pi's forehead and seared her into a cold panic. Hunger cut with desperation oozed through claw-like paws that stretched across the water with the hopes of snaring powerless prey. On the left fork their beastly brethren kept their hunger at bay as they gnawed through metal cans using razor sharp teeth that cut like a jagged knife through butter.

The current pulled Pi to the left where hundreds of hungry teeth chomped with anticipation. Closer and closer she drew towards mouths filled with black and pointy teeth, blood-red tongues and throats scarred from sharp bones that had been swallowed whole. Ferocious and hungry, angry and rabid, the pack fought for the right to have Pi between their jaws. Two hairless creatures with pocked faces and abscessed skin that oozed blood and pus, were intent on getting to her first.

"Get it Richard, get it!"

"Hold on Paul, it's not close enough yet."

Three of their rivals leapt from a rusted pipe that hung loosely from the sewer ceiling and plunged into the water.

"Go after them Richard. It's getting away."

"I'm not going in there again. My sores are killing me and that water burns like a flaming torch."

The three who plunged for Pi fought to catch her as the current sped fast around the corner. The smallest of the three yelled out as he treaded water, "It's mine, you greedy bastards. You ate yesterday."

"Too bad you're not gonna' eat again today petite frite." His two elder cousins flicked their tails snapping him in the face. Weak from an empty stomach he swallowed a bucketful of water and sank under the surface.

"Bon, he's finally gone. One less mouth to think about."

"Shut the hell up and get it now."

"Who made you the boss? You're not the boss of me. You shut up."

"What did you say?"

"Oh, now you're deaf too. What an idiot. I said, you are not the boss of me."

"You calling me an idiot? You were named after Monsieur idiot himself. Your father is Monsieur idiot, idiot."

"That's it! I've endured years of your abuse I will stand for it no longer."

"What are you going to do about it, idiot?"

As they argued, streams of rainwater poured through metal slots in the sewer's roof. A downpour fell upon the arguing cousins and plunged them to unknown depths. As they sank out of sight the remainder of their lives floated and trailed to the surface in the form of broken bubbles.

Pi traveled through endless corridors and dark passageways bumping and scraping jagged stonewalls. Far above her head the streets of the city vibrated. Avenue Louis Roche, rue Louis Calmel, and avenue de Stalingrad. She passed under l'avenue Jean Jaurès, twisted and turned through tunnels under the Forêt de Saint-Germain-en-Laye. She was carried under small towns and villages; Andrésy, Boisemont, Hardricourt, Juzlers, Mantes-la-Joile, Bennecourt and finally just north of Limetz-Villez where the tunnel narrowed and rose to ground level. The walls closed in and the brick and rock tunnel turned to metal. The narrow walls increased the water pressure and shot Pi out like a cannon ball through a tiny opening in a rusted pipe. She laid splayed on the banks of a small tributary to the Siene in a bed of wet twigs, leaves, and soft grass.

Chapter 9

PI ROSE QUICKLY, shook the water from her feathers and ran to safety under the cover of fallen and twisted oak branches. She caught her breath and noticed a father goose and his eight goslings that waddled along the river in search of their morning meal. The two youngest gamboled through the tall grasses, oblivious to the importance of their father's task and responsibilities. His young charges patched in coffee and chocolate-colored feathers, sifted through dew-covered grass in search of seeds and insects. Pi observed them from a natural blind and memories flushed her with warmth and longing for her own family back on des Champs Élyséses.

She left the father and his children to graze in peace and walked through a blanket of farmland covered in thick rows of Brussels sprouts, green cabbage and thick-leafed lettuce. Field collected rain mixed with soil turned out large clumps of mud, some so big they met the height of Pi's shoulders. She wove her way through rocky ribbons of mud balls; anthills, gravel mounds, and shards of rusted metal that spilled out onto a furrow lined with feathery absinthiums, blue bellworts, drooping lilies of the valley and mustard doused yellow rockets. The flowery path led her to a vast, moist and lush forest, and in the center of the forest a glassy pond shimmered and beckoned.

Pi's faced filled with wonder as she stepped further into the forest. With each press of her foot to the moist and rich soil, colors rose to the surface from deep below. The print of her left foot released blushes of lavender and slices of pink-orange. Her right yielded flakes of wisteria mixed with berries of blue and purple. Everywhere she walked, rainbows of colors exploded and painted the earth. Water lilies floated on the surface of the pond like leafy saucers. Their long lily legs tiptoed ever so slowly across the murky bottom, pushing with the tip of just one toe. Cerulean-colored frogs hitched and hopped their way from lily to lily in hopes of snaring unsuspecting morning midges.

"What is this place? It is so beautiful and the air so sweet."

Lulled by the sway and twist of the lilies, she was brought to the entrance of a cave with a small and jagged opening. She hesitated and inspected the dull grey stone above the chiseled aperture. Curiosity got the better of her and she proceeded through the cave's only entrance.

The sound of water that dripped into a pool echoed from the walls, along with fragments of voices from deep within the cave. Her heart thumped loudly as she peered into the darkness. It was pitch black. She cocked her head left, then right, attempting to hone her hearing.

"He was trouble. Nothing but…"

"Yessiree, he was… indeed…"

"Con permiso…you…"

As she walked deeper into the cave the wind whipped and whistled and wrapped an invisible and eerie cloak around her neck. Something grabbed her leg. "What's that?!" It gave a slight tug and then vanished. "That's enough. I'm going back." She ran towards the light of the cave's opening, the pond and lilies insight. And then, another something slithered through her legs and lassoed her. She fell to the ground and was dragged back deeper into the cave. She fought her captor with claws dug into the rock and dirt and flapped her wings but to no avail. Whatever had her in its grip wouldn't let go and just as she stopped squirming and fighting, her head collided with a large rock.

"What did you catch today, Quick Jac?" Darkhana, a small Chaffinch with two mustard-colored patches on her shoulders and ochre colored feathers on her head, hopped closer to see what Quick Jac had brought in.

Jac Carlson, otherwise known as Quick Jac, came from the great, big and wide-open expanse of the American West. A red-bellied woodpecker with a tongue twice as long as any other was one of the first to come to France during the last great escape of immigrants, and the first to inhabit the cave. He spent his first two years alone fending off any and all intruders with the power of his strong and extraordinarily long tongue. Brash and hard driving with eyes sharp and precise, it was impossible to lie to him. Judge and jury, he kept the scales of reality and opinion in balance.

Quick Jac unfurled his tongue and Pi rolled out like a sweet candied gift. "I'd say we have a female who's under-weight, over-exercised and far from home."

"How do you know?" Darkhana asked even though she knew the answer.

"When you've rustled as many unwanted visitors as I have you know the signs. Everybody tells a story. Look at the shape of her legs; too scrawny for her age. And take a gander at those feathers, they're all floppy-jawed and dry."

"How long will she be out for?"

"Aw, I didn't put much of a stranglehold on her. She should be back in a minute or two. Once we listen to her sob story we'll toss her out like the rest of 'em."

Darkhana identified with the bird who lay at her feet. A wisp of sadness and loss emanated from her small beak. She recognized something in the bird that she had once possessed. She too had left her home, Turkmenistan, looking for a better life. No one knows for sure exactly what her life was like before she arrived at the cave but it's safe to say that it wasn't very pleasant. The only time Darkhana spoke of life growing up in the little southwestern village of Ak-Dashayak was when previous cave dwellers began asking her questions. "I will tell you only that life was very difficult and many times unfair," she told them twelve years ago when coming to the cave. She had a sad softness and a lulling lilt in her voice. When she spoke, the rhythm of swaying bay leaves in a spring breeze could be heard. "Messieurs, I have had my fair share of wrongs done to me. I could tell you more but ah…there is nothing more to say."

At first, the all-male group of cave dwellers refused to allow Darkhana into their community, but after hearing her sing an aria of protestation, the hardened men of the cave collapsed and wept for hours, having never heard anything so sweet, so lulling, so beautiful.

"Maybe we should see who she is and where she came from." Darkhana suggested trying to influence Quick Jac to be gentle. "Maybe she is the 'real McCoy' as you call them. Maybe she is one of us?"

"You've said that before Miss Darkhana and we ain't heard not one poor bronco's story yet that was the real McCoy. You should know by now that most of 'em just want some free grub and a place to bed down."

"You're probably right Quick Jac, however, something says that this one's different."

"Are you getting soft on me Darkhana?"

"No, I just think that we could afford her the benefit of the doubt before we kick her out."

As Darkahana and Quick Jac discussed Pi's fate, a broad-chested checkered pigeon came out of the darkness deep from within the cave. Señor Lafargue carried around the weight of all his regrets and should-have-dones on his round and now drooped shoulders. The by-product of hauling his load for so many years was a compressed and squat body with frayed and tattered feathers. Head on, Señor Lafargue looked liked a splintered water barrel lumbering about on short, thin, and bowed legs. His beak, long, bumpy and bruised, looked like a rotten Yucca fruit.

"Como es?" He asked upon seeing Pi's lifeless body.

"We're sorry Señor Lafargue, did we wake you?"

"It is okay Darkhana, I was supposed to be up long ago." Referring to Pi he asked, "What do we have here?"

"Probably just another grub rustler." Quick Jac never gave anyone the benefit of proving himself otherwise. He always assumed and assumed correctly, that those who had come to the cave came only to take and never to give. He didn't have to say much to an uninvited visitor. After having a taste of being rolled up in his long and sticky tongue they didn't' need much help fleeing the cave.

Señor Lafargue inspected Pi by listening to her breath. "Hmm, she seems to have a special soul. Maybe she's been sent to us especial."

"Not you too? Lafargue, tuck in your Spanish. Let's just see what she has to say for herself." Quick Jac stabbed Pi's chest with the long claw of his right foot. She muttered something incomprehensible and fell silent.

"Quick Jac, don't be so rough." Darkahana pushed her way past him and Senor Lafargue. "Başkalarına içine sopa önce nasıl incittiğini görmek için kendinize iğne sopa."

"Drop the Turk, Darkhana and speak somethin' I can understand."

"I said, stick the needle in yourself to see how it hurts before you stick it into others."

"What the heck does that mean?"

"Be easy on her."

Señor Lafargue smiled at the familiar jab of difference that kept Darkahna and Quick Jac on equal footing. "Ay Dios. Give the poor little one a chance to speak for herself and then we can decide what we do with her."

"Should we not wait for Gritty Grimy Gramps so we can all hear her story?" Darkhana asked.

"I saw him leave just before sunrise sayin' he wanted some chopped veggies for breakfast. "I need some greens for my hygiene," is what he said." Quick Jac scratched his chest and shook his head. "You vegetarians kill me."

Gritty Grimy Gramps' name only partially described his deportment. With regard to his personal cleanliness, he was anything but gritty and grimy. That moniker originated from his fierce sense of independence that was self-fostered from an early age. As far as the "Gramps" goes, he earned that by the age of eleven months after numerous attempts by his mother, father, sisters and brothers failed to inspire him to get off his tail and do something with his life besides sleeping all day in the crook of a swaying Taluto tree. "Your grandfather is more athletic and enthusiastic than you are," his mother admonished. "You act like you're the old man." Gritty Grimy Gramps would then groan and turn his head away from his domineering mother. "Fine! Lie in that tree for the rest of your life for all I care," she snapped. "We're taking a hike through the forest!" The young Palawan Peacock simply moaned and rolled over as his family walked deep into the island's thick and abundant flora. That was the last time he saw them alive. Within a matter of minutes a typhoon whacked the island with a great whoosh that swept away anything and everyone that wasn't firmly rooted. Gritty's perceived laziness saved him from the powerful and devastating storm as he clung with determination to the crook of that rooted Taluto tree.

"I agree with Darkhana. We should wait for Gramps. He would want to…"

Pi started to stir with the last of Señor Lafargue's words. She moved her head from side to side as if trying to shake loose imaginary pebbles between her ears.

"Right on time," Quick Jac declared. "She's wakin' up. You two stand back case she gets ratty." He inspected Pi with the tip of his sensitive tongue. "Nope, false alarm. She's out again."

Senor Lafargue stepped in closer to Pi. "She has had some time of it."

"Who hasn't Lafargue?" Quick Jac countered then spun on his heels. The sound of something being swept on the ground echoed its way back from the front of the cave. "He's back."

Scuffed sounds, like that of a long and heavy overcoat being dragged, echoed from the cave's entrance. Proceeded by thin, narrow rays of colored light that beamed from an unseen prism that bounced and shimmered off the quartz walls. A two-footed lopsided stride preceded the dragging and reverberated through the cave until shimmering green and gold crest feathers could be seen. Gritty Grimy Gramps' bark was as ferocious as his bite, which didn't quite match his peacock beauty and grandeur. He spoke as if he had a bunch of wet stones in his beak causing his words to spit and sputter from his mouth like kernels of corn being popped on an open flame.

"What the heck is this crap?" He peered at Pi and then spread the entirety of his feathers across the cave walls.

"Gramps, would you mind foldin' those things up? It's dark enough in here without you blockin' what's left."

Gritty Grimy Gramps didn't like that Quick Jac was the cock of the cave, telling him what to do but he knew that Jack could out match him one-on-one in speed alone. He slowly tucked his fanned feathers of iridescent eyes until they draped his back and swept the moist ground behind his tail. "So what is it?"

"'It' is a she," Darkhana said with a dash of annoyance.

"Looks like another runaway who stumbled onto us. I was gonna get rid of her as soon as I found her, but I holstered myself and convinced Darkhana to wait until you got back."

Quick Jac didn't even bother to look at the incredulous scowl on Darkhana's face.

"Jack, get her up and out."

"Hold your horses Gramps. Lafargue, put a foot on her tail in case she puts up a fight."

"Señor Quick Jac, I don't think we need to hold her down. I told you, she's a gentle soul."

"He's right," Darkhana added. Just get on with it. She's not going to hurt anyone."

Quick Jac unfurled his tongue and coiled it around Pi's neck and flipped her to her feet. Her head snapped from her chest and bounced off her back and then onto her chest again. He then flicked his lightning-fast tongue so that the tip balanced Pi's head perpendicular to her feet. She woke with a start and looked around at the creatures staring at her as if she were caged in a store window.

"Who are you? Where am I?"

"It's you that needs to be answering the questions." Gritty Grimy Gramps strode around Pi inspecting her like a prison warden.

"You're trespassing young lady and we don't take kindly to trespassers," Quick Jac added as he retracted his tongue. "What brought you here and where did you come from?"

Darkhana boldly stood next to Pi and addressed her cave mates. "Gentlemen, why don't you give our guest a little space so that she can answer your questions without the intimidation?"

Pi looked to Darkhana. "Yes, a little bit of space would be nice, messieurs."

Quick Jac and Gritty Grimy Gramps reluctantly moved aside. Señor Lafargue stood off to one side quietly observing like a teacher watching his favorite student take a test he knew she was well prepared for.

"Merci messieurs. I have traveled quite a long way and to save time and the retelling of my overly repeated story, I have walked all this way from Paris."

Gritty Grimy Gramps harrumphed, "That's about as believable as an honest aristocrat."

"She does look like a grilse after swimming up stream too long," Quick Jac chuckled.

"Pardonnez-moi monsieur, I did not catch your name."

"Quick Jac's the name, taming the wild is my game."

"And you sir?" Pi asked Gritty Grimy Gramps.

"Just call me Gramps."

"Monsieur Quick Jac, monsieur Gramps, I am anything but dishonest. I stumbled upon your home purely by accident when the lilies in your pond led me to your door."

Simultaneously, Quick Jac and Gritty Grimy Gramps exploded with laughter. Darkhana and Señor Lafargue didn't crack a smile. They let the fools be foolish.

Gritty Grimy Gramps caught his breath and said, "You're nothing but a rootless wanderer. That's all you have? That's the best you can do little lady?"

Quick Jac added, "Whadda ya have one, maybe two songs in your repertoire? That ain't nothin'. On a bad day I can call up forty-two different tunes."

Gritty Grimy Gramps fanned his feathers and peered down at Pi. "The depths of hell should be lined with the likes of your kind. Now get the hell out of our cave!"

Pi's face flushed with anger and for the first time contempt. She erupted with all the might and force that had accumulated in her small body from the start of her journey. "Messieurs, whatever you might think, I am not rootless! Everything that I am, all that I might ever become is firmly rooted atop l'Arc de Triomphe with my family, the Phillecroix' and if you are not familiar with or lack the brain capacity to retain the name then imprint it now! P-H-I-L-L-E-C-R-O-I-X, Phillecroix. And make no mistake I am "rooted" no matter where I may be!"

The two cave dwellers stood speechless. They easily could

have taken Pi down with a quick jab from one of their sharply pointed talons but they were impressed with her veracity and zeal.

Señor Lafargue and Darkhana were equally impressed and extremely delighted. Never before had anyone spoken to Quick Jac and Gritty Grimy Gramps in the way she just did. Señor Lafargue stepped next to Pi and addressed Quick Jac and Gramps with newfound confidence and authority. "Amigos, I think we should listen to the señorita, yes?"

Darkhana could feel the shift of power take place in the cave for the first time since she arrived. "Yes amigos, Señor Lafargue is right. Show your respect for our guest."

Gritty Grimy Gramps begrudgingly folded his feathers. "Oui mademoiselle, I will remember. 'Phillecroix.' Pardon my ignorance."

Pi relaxed her stance and shoulders. The intensity slowly left her body and her eyes softened. "Merci."

"Pardon mam' but did you say Phillecroix?"

"Yes, that is correct monsieur Quick Jac."

"Who the hell is Phillecroix?" Grumbled Gramps.

"You mean to tell me Gramps that you've never heard of the famous Phillecroix family?"

"No, I haven't Jac."

"Well they're easily the best flying family for the last three-hundred years or more. Why they…"

"Excuse me, Jac," Darkhana quickly and gracefully interrupted. Quick Jac was taken by surprise upon hearing half his name spoken by Darkhana. He gave her a look of warning but she paid him no attention. "Mademoiselle, if I may?"

"Yes, of course."

"Merci. Gentleman, the Phillecroix family is as much a part of ornithological history as is the Great Avian Revolution. Mademoiselle Pi's ancestry is quite notable in their bravery, dedication to country, and their athletic abilities. If you bothered to look you would have noticed the blue streak running down her chest. A sure sign of her lineage."

"Well I'll be! I thought that streak looked familiar. Pardon me mam, I had no idea. Your father and grandfather were legends in the States. Why they…"

Pi slowly dropped her head to her chest.

"Sorry mam, did I say somethin' I shouldn't have?"

"Non, It's just that I have come all this way because…well to hear you describe him…well…I am extremely tired…Thank you Darkhanna for speaking so highly of our family. I could not have said it better myself."

Señor Lafargue gently said, "I think we should give our guest a little time to rest her tired legs."

"Well yes, of course." "I was thinking the same thing. Why do you talk so much?"

"Me, are you kidding? You're the one who's…"

"Gentleman, gentleman, please. Let's not add more din to the echo." Darkhana turned her attention to Pi. "Mademoiselle, we humbly request that you stay the evening as our honored guest. Wherever you journey takes you, let us and our modest home provide you with a bit of comfort and respite until you are prepared to set out again." Darkhana turned to Quick Jac and Gritty Grimy Gramps instructing them with a look to agree.

"Yes, of course you're welcome. It's not everyday that we are so hospitable but since you are here…"

"What Gramps is trying to say…"

"Merci Darkhana. I think I know what he is trying to convey. I am honored Gramps that you would allow me to be a guest in your home."

"If the others are okay with it then who am I to argue? Stay as long as you like. Just don't get in my feathers."

"Non, of course not." Pi tucked a smile just behind her beak and turned to Señor Lafargue. "Señor Lafargue, would you please be so kind as to show me where I can rest my tired legs?"

"Of course. But first, let us glide with the lilies and watch the meteor showers. We have such a good picture of the sky from the lily pond. We will float on the water that carries to the River Epte. Come señorita, we will float under the stars and have our crowns tickled by weeping willows and wondering wisterias."

"I will make up a place for you to sleep mademoiselle. Enjoy yourself. Señor Lafargue is a very good tour guide."

"Merci Darkhana."

Señor Lafargue extended his right wing and made his best attempt to bow majestically. "Shall we mademoiselle?"

The light outside the cave was filled with colors stitched into the late day sky. Gold and amber, puffs of pinks and reds along with hues of purple waved through the sky like a quilt blowing in the wind. The willows, as promised wept and the wisterias dangled, together keeping watch over the pond.

"Let's set in here."

Señor Lafargue walked to the edge of the pond, tucked his legs and slid into the shimmering water. "Ah, perfecto! You see what I learned from the red-headed ducks? Now you try."

Pi stepped close to the water's edge, sat in the cool dirt and pushed her weight forward until she too was bobbing effortlessly atop the lily pond.

"You see, this is nice."

"Yes, Señor Lafargue, this is very nice. I haven't had much time lately to float in cool and calm waters like these."

"You have been traveling for a long time, yes?"

"A very long time it seems, and I don't know how I am going to continue tomorrow. I didn't know that it was going to be so difficult." Her brave mask began to crumble. "Señor Lafargue, please, tell me how you came to France."

Señor Lafargue gave no hesitation to Pi's invitation; there hadn't been an interesting soul-filled traveler to the cave before her arrival in many, many years.

"Si. I have heard of the great land of France and the wonderful music here and though it doesn't have the beat I grew up with in Cuba, the music is excellente!" He leaned in close and said confidentially, "Sometimes, in my sleep I hear music from my country and I want to fly to my homeland on the back of the notes.

"Monsieur Lafargue, I too long to hear the music of Paris…I have so many questions I wish to ask you. Until now I have never traveled far from my home. I wish that I could fly to your country and all the countries of the world. I would fly…I would fly…"

"Flying is not everything senorita. More important is what you see from where you see it. Your journey is important. When I fly, por cierto, I can see many things from the air but I cannot see the same things that you can see from walking on the soil and streets and fields and beaches."

"Yes, this is true I suppose. But tell me please, about Cuba. Tell me about the birds and the food and the smells that I have heard lace the air."

"Senorita, are you sure you want to get an old and lonely man talking about his homeland?"

"Yes, I do, very much Señor Larfague."

"Okay. Una condición por favor. You call me Ernesto."

"Very well, Ernesto."

"Gracias mi amiga. There was a time when you could smell beans cooking in big, open metal pots and sip sweet water ice and peck leftover foods at the baseball games. Oh, the baseball games!" His eyes began to well with tears as he recalled happy days spent at Estadio del Havana. "Entonces, neustro." He caught himself speaking Spanish and recoiled his words back onto his tongue as quickly as a frog catches a buzzing fly. "Sorry senorita, I sometimes forget where I am. It's all this talk about the ole' country that brings out my native language."

"Señor Lafargue? Ernesto, your language is very pleasing.

It sounds like your words are dancing out into the air. Some of them sound French."

"Ah yes, but if it is a dance that you hear when I speak then I speak with two left feet, where you and your country dance a beautiful waltz."

Pi smiled and a small laugh bubbled through her nostrils.

"You see, I do sound funny?"

"Non, not at all. Please, tell me more about Cuba."

"Entonces, we had the best seat in the ballpark, above the plate at home, on top of the lights. They were free in those days too. You didn't pay the gulls like you do now. And we talked or better I should say, we argued. We argued a lot before and after every game. This sent our sangre boiling and our faces as red as an August sunset. Many times our arguing turned into fighting and many feathers were pecked out of our heads." He paused as the memory nipped him.

"What is it Ernesto?"

"Adios mios. I was just thinking how so much time has gone. I feel so much sadness now when I speak words that go with the película en mi cabeza."

Pi cocked her head slightly.

"There, you see? I've done it again. En francias, la cinema… Excusz-moi…ma tete esta…Oh, you see. I am just an old stupid bird. I have tried for so many years to learn your beautiful language and every time I mix up las verbas con…You see! I did it again."

Pi looked at Ernesto in the same way she did when her father told her stories of his heroic days flying for the Resistance. Her eyes became soft, moist, delicate and loving. Ernesto's heart started to melt around its edges; he was touched and a bit smitten as well. Now, just like Paul Phillecroix, he too was committed to do anything this precious princess would ask of him.

"Que pasa, Senorita?"

"Nothing, nothing at all Señor. Please, tell me more."

Ernesto talked long into the night and told Pi of the day that he decided to leave his family and beautiful island home. He described the horrible scene that took place when he told family and flock of his decision to leave and how desperately he tried in vain to convince them to escape with him in the middle of the night. He feared for their lives and he knew that life on the little island would never be the same. Many birds would need to die just so that one little bird who thought he was bigger and smarter than the other birds would come to power and how this little-big bird told all the island's flocks how he would take care of them and provide for them and that they would never have to worry about going hungry or sick. But, Ernesto heard something different coming far from the other side of this little-big bird's beak and it talked at the same time but it said something different and if you didn't listen as carefully as Ernesto had you would be fooled and only hear the words coming out one side of his beak and believe everything it told you.

"You know Pi, we are a very proud bunch of birds and we never like to say that we are wrong about anything, but oh how I wish that I was wrong about that little-big bird."

She noticed the tears he was choking back and reached out her left wing. "Do you want to tell me about it Ernesto?"

"I don't want to trouble you with an old man's regrets."

"Ernesto, I want you to tell me, s'il vous plaît."

He started off in a long slow cadence. "It began with the meetings. He called them the "Los Reuniones por la Personas," the Meetings for the Peoples. These meetings took place far outside of the town center near the sugar cane fields where we were hidden beneath the thick stalks. The little-big bird did not have so much power yet and the birds that controlled the flocks wanted him dead or alive, as long as he was out of the way and not spreading his words of trouble and change. But you see the little-big bird was smart, for as stupid as he was, because he knew how to entertain the flocks with the way he strutted and shook his tail feathers and with that two-sided beak of his."

With the telling of the story, Ernesto's determination of his youth returned and he held his head high and pushed out his chest. "It was not so long after I went to some of the meetings that I knew that this little-big bird was full of very hot air and held by many strings. He said that as a nación of birds we must rise up and conquer what he called "oppression and dishonesty." The little-big bird would talk and shout for hours under the swaying sugar canes and many believed and helped him in his mission to seize the birds that held the power of the flocks. He succeeded in his hunt to be top bird, and there was much celebración. His birds pecked and chewed at the sugar canes that once kept his words from floating far away."

"What happened Ernesto? What happened after he took over the flocks?"

A brief wind whipped off the pond and carried with it a calling from the past. The wind draped over Ernesto's round and fallen shoulders like a beaded lead shawl. His entire demeanor shrank under the added weight. Like a piece of withered and rotten driftwood he sat motionless.

"Señor Ernesto, are you alright?"

"Lo siento. I am sorry. Something came over me which I had not felt or remembered in a long time." He waddled his weight from one side of his body to the other trying to alleviate the arthritis that had plagued him for the last several years.

"My friend, it became very awful. At first, because everyone was so happy: singing and dancing in the streets. I thought that maybe I was wrong about the little-big bird. Maybe my homing sense went loco and everyone knew the truth but me. Then after the drunkenness of the 'something new' wore off and everyone left the parties and parades and went back to their lives it all went mal. So bad, so very quickly.

"The little-big bird became restless. Falling prey to his own power he did reckless attacks with his hombres. They went up to the sun and then dove back down with sharpened beaks into flocks of blameless squabs with their las madres y los padres. He was now called, "Dos alas de terror" the two-winged terror and everyone was afraid of him and his birds, so afraid that no one would stand up to him and say that this life is not better than what he had before. No, this is the same bird with just different colored feathers.

"Had I more courage I could have done something. I could have shaken my tail feathers, I could have spoken louder than the little-big bird, I could have…I have committed a pecado grande. After all these years it is me who is the pecador; the sinner."

He turned his head away embarrassed by the tears streaming down his face. Guilt had taken such a toll on Ernesto that it had eaten away at the fragments of his self-esteem. He felt it coming on and followed it into the future and still didn't have the head to do anything about it.

"You are not a pécheur. You are not sinner. You warned the flock and they did not hear you. How could you have known that the little-big bird was so evil and destructive? It was impossible for you to have known. You can not blame yourself anymore than sunflowers can blame themselves for not lifting their down turned faces skyward after heavy rains."

Ernesto turned his head slowly towards Pi and asked, "You are a philosopher too?"

"Señor Ernesto," Pi stated with much respect. "I have learned something very important from you today. Even if you do not believe it to be true, your story has had a great effect on me. I am grateful for our meeting."

His eyes flickered a long burned out flame. "Gracias chica but it is I who has learned something from you."

"You have?"

"Yes. I have learned just by looking into your eyes that I have been treating myself with much falta de respeto."

She searched him for an explanation.

"Ah sorry, I mean disrespect. I have come many miles on my own. It took much strength. It was not easy but I'm not el muerto. There's more life in me if I decide to live it as if I were still alive and not dead!"

Pi took a step backwards and tucked her wings behind her as she lowered her head. "I bow to you Señor Ernesto, you are royalty. How do you say king in Español?"

"El Rey."

"To you, el Rey de los Cielos, I bow my head and pay homage to a bird with great courage."

Ernesto was flattened with gratitude. He had waited for all the days of his life to receive such a gracious gift of validation and here in this remote place with the painted skies, weeping trees and walking lilies, all it took was a gesture as small as a sand fly. "Gracias, Pi. Muchas gracias."

"Just because I say something does not mean that I follow my own words."

"You are, how do you say…ah, yes, you are très intelligent." There was a pause of silence as they flipped their feet in unison. "Are you ready to go back now and get some sleep mademoiselle?"

"Oui, I am very ready."

The unassuming friends floated gently back to the cave's entrance taking in each and every detail of each and every tree and flower that surrounded the pond.

"You will sleep well now my friend. The water has magical powers that have seeped into your feathers and will protect and calm you through the night. And if that is not enough, if the night greets you with fear, I will be near to help you."

"Señor Ernesto, you are perhaps one of the kindest, most wonderful birds that I have ever known, except for my father, of course."

"Your father is the reason you have traveled so far, yes?"

"Yes."

"I see…well, he is the lucky one to have a daughter like you." He puffed out his chest and crossed his right wing across his breast and said, "Senorita, I have re-opened a piece of my heart that has not been ocupado in a very long time. Now, you will live there forever."

"Señor Ernesto, although I have very few friends I will always remember you."

This time he didn't attempt to hide the tears that welled in his eyes. "Muchas gracias. Muchas gracias."

A night without dreams is a night with complete peace. Of all places to have found such a tranquil and restful night in this damp cave of runaways and strays that long ago lost their way.

In the morning, Gritty Grimy Gramps stood by the opening of the cave spreading his feathers. Darkness swept across Pi's face.

"Who's there?"

"It's Gramps. Sorry if I woke you but you should be getting up now anyway." He tucked his wings and the cave filled with morning light. "It's none of my business but I have to ask, have you ever thought of asking someone to go to your destination for you? To fly there instead of you walking?"

She flirted with a smile. "Are you offering your services monsieur Gramps?"

"Well, I might have in my younger days been of great service to you, but now these old wings…well anyway…I apologize for my behavior last night."

"Don't. I understand."

"Your family is very fortunate to have each other. I wish that I had the opportunity to live my life over again. I would have done things very differently. Ah, the ignorance of my youth." He kicked the dirt with his left foot. "I'm still paying for my mistakes."

"Monsieur Gramps, I am sure that no matter what choices you had made when you were young you probably would have regretted some of them later."

"I suppose so. Still, I miss my mother and I should have…"

"What's all the noise?" From out of the shadows Quick Jac appeared followed by Darkhana. "For crying our loud, can't I ever get some good shut-eye?"

"I'm sorry if we woke you monsieur Quick Jac."

"Don't even bother apologizing to him," Gramps said. "He complains if he sleeps and complains if he doesn't."

"Look who's calling the feather frayed? You're about as cantankerous as a three-legged lizard."

Pi looked over at Darkhana who motioned her head towards the cave entrance. She and Pi slowly walked out leaving Quick Jac and Gritty Grimy Gramps arguing.

"It's better out here, yes?"

"Do they always bicker with each other like that?"

"Everyday."

"How is it living with them?"

"They may bicker and argue but underneath all their crustiness lays decency."

"I'm sure that's true. I've had the pleasure of seeing some of Gramp's tenderness."

"You'll be leaving us now?"

"Yes."

"I've enjoyed having you here."

"Merci."

"Do you think you might ever be back this way again?"

"I don't know Darkhana but I hope that we do meet again."

"Yes, that would be nice." She looked up towards the sky. "I will keep good thoughts for you Pi."

"And I you. Would you please say goodbye to the others and tell them thank you?"

She walked away from Darkhana down the path she came from just the day before. She learned that looking back only makes it that much harder to say goodbye.

"Pi?" Darkhana called.

Pi stopped but did not turn to look at Darkhana. "Oui?"

"Can I come with you?"

Pi smiled, took a deep breath and then turned to face Darkhana. "Je suis désolé."

"Yes, I suppose you are right."

"You can leave anytime you like."

"If only it were that easy."

"It is. Au revoir Darkhana. Bon chance.

"Goodbye Pi. Good luck." Darkhana lazily turned her head towards the cave and abruptly turned back to Pi. "Pi! Wait! Don't you want to say goodbye to Señor Ernesto?"

"Non, merci. I can't. Please give him my regrets and tell him that perhaps one day we shall meet in his beloved Cuba."

Pi stepped further away from the cave. Her walk rolled into a slow jog, which turned into a run. She sprinted out of the forest and back to the banks of the river.

Chapter 10

The River Seine forked right near les Mousseaux. Runoff from sandstone, gravel and sugar deposits have built along the brown soil shores for centuries. Footing is uncertain and dangerous. One should always be concerned about being swept away with the current when approaching the riverbank.

Pi had walked through thick grasses, fields of corn, soybeans and sprouts and traveled further today than any other. She had covered a great distance since leaving Darkhana and the others at the cave. She felt fortified by Ernesto and Darkhana's friendship and hoped to see them again one day.

A loud thrashing emanated from the river over Pi's left shoulder. She turned and saw a creature of immense size - at least fifteen feet long. It whipped itself back and forth from side to side in an attempt to free itself from an unseen captor. She ran to the distressed beast that was asparagus green in color with razor sharp scales running down its back. Two long, pointy tentacles stuck out from each side of its head. A large eye ringed in pink peered out from just below the surface of the river. Its tail was as tall as a seven-masted schooner and its fins equal in width.

Pi had heard tall tales of the Giant Sea Fish but never thought them to be any more than that —fantastical stories with no facts. Now, she was face to face with it. The more it struggled for freedom the more entrenched it became.

At the river's edge, Pi tested the depth. There was a dark, swirling pool of water that surrounded the Giant Sea Fish and she hesitated before stepping in. The creature's right eye caught sight of her and pleaded, "Please…help me. Aidez-moi s'il vous plaît."

"What can I do?" She asked frantically.

"I need…water…on…" He desperately tried to communicate but he couldn't breathe.

"What, what do you need me to do?"

"Fan some…water on my…gills."

Pi took a deep breath and plunged into the swirling pool. Trapped on a sandbar, the creature cupped his gigantic tail around Pi preventing the river from sweeping her away.

"Good. Now use your wings to fan…"

"Oui, I understand."

Flapping her wings intermittently she created a stream of water that cascaded onto the Giant Sea Fish. "Are you breathing okay now?"

"Yes, that's it. It's working." The oxygenated water renewed him and was helping to break down the sandbar. "Yes, yes, you're loosening up the sand too. I can…almost break free." With each wing of water the mound of sand began to dissolve into the river and just as he was about to be freed a torrent of water flushed him and Pi out into the center of the river sending them south towards Paris. Mud, salt and sand filled Pi's ears, eyes, nose and lungs as the river tossed and turned her head over tail. All she could hear was gurgling and popping and swooshing of water. "I can't breathe…it's all…"

The gurgling and popping and swooshing sounds stopped. The torrent abated. The Giant Sea Fish righted himself and flipped Pi to the shore with his large tail. She lay motionless in the tall grass, her chest scarcely rising to the faint call of her lungs to take air. From his place in the river the Giant Sea Fish watched hopelessly.

"Precious bird, please wake."

Hoping for a miracle, he circled around and around creating a small eddy near the shoreline. Rich oxygen percolated up from the riverbed to the water's surface turning into tiny bubbles that grew to larger bubbles that the wind then carried high into the Norman sky. As the bubbles ascended they grew larger and larger, rounder and rounder until the entire countryside was enveloped in one plump, glossy bubble. The sky above the bubble quickly grew dark grey and silver, and one by one raindrops plunged down onto the big bubble which repelled the raindrops and bounced them back into the Upper Sky, creating voluminous energy that pressed, packed and shaped itself into a lightning bolt the length of the River itself. The Upper Sky pulled back its enormous arm across the Channel to the coast of England and hurled the red-hot lightning bolt through the bubbled sky. In an attosecond the bolt landed beside Pi's lifeless body igniting the tall grasses into a raging wall of fire that encircled her. The flames grew taller and taller and hotter and hotter. The Giant Sea Fish watched hopelessly from the river until he couldn't stand to watch any longer. With a great burst of power he beat his tail against the river driving waves of water onto the raging fire. Over and over he tried dousing the flame with river water until he was near exhaustion. With only one heart beat left the flames began to subside. The bubbles high above burst and rain poured down on the river valley extinguishing the fire. Thousands of spits of water from the bursting bubbles sprayed far and wide like a giant heavenly sprinkler. Tiny droplets fell to earth falling on Pi, lightly pricking her face, head and chest. They seeped into her feathers, down their quills and beneath her skin spreading renewed energy and in instant, she was flung upright onto her feet. Each and every one of her more than four thousand feathers stood at attention. Her blue breast streak sparked and flashed while her tail flipped towards the back of her head.

"Fish?!" She screamed. "Fish?!"

In the river under an overhang of the shoreline just beneath the surface, the Giant Sea Fish lay on its side. His gill chambers barely operating. Like a sluggish valve they'd opened, paused then paused again before opening.

"Fish! Fish! Mon Dieu." She swept the river with her eyes searching for the Giant Sea Fish – south then north, across from side to side.

Crestfallen, she tucked her legs and sat on the moist soil, feeling lost and alone. Everything around her lost its wholeness, its depth, its weight, and its color was barren and lonely. She rested her head on her chest and stared into the rippling river and there just beneath the surface she saw the Giant Sea Fish's great tail.

"Fish, fish, you're alive." She tried to wake him with her left wing but she couldn't reach. Desperate she dug one claw into the soft soil and slid her body off the precipice and pressed the tip of her right wing into the Giant Sea Fish's body. When he didn't respond she clawed him with her long front claw and shook him with every ounce of her strength. Blood began to pool and rose to the river's surface and floated there. She tried to remove her claw but it was in too deep, embedded below his razor-like scales. She pulled and shook and tried to free her leg but to know avail. "Merde!" The pools of blood grew larger and linked together like rose petals. Pi saw her reflection in the glossy plasma. She screamed and shivered in fear and disgust and in her panic her claw ripped out of the Giant Sea Fish. The force threw her entire body away from the edge of the riverbank.

"Mon dieu." She ran back to see the bubble of blood drifting down stream and the Giant Sea Fish staring at her with two full bright and alert eyes.

"Fish, are you alright?"

"Oui mademoiselle, I am good. Come to think of it, I am better than good. I feel like I have new blood running through my body. I feel like I can swim faster than ever before. Watch this!" He darted out of sight and leapt high out of the water into the air, then dove back under the current and in a flash he appeared at Pi's feet.

"Did you see that?! I can't believe it. Did you see?! Whales and swordfish look out! I don't know what you did mademoiselle but I thank you. Merci, merci, merci!"

"I didn't do anything, I am just so happy that you are alive. I thought that…"

"You thought that I was dead? Oh non, non, non, non. We fish have an amazing ability to hibernate on command. It really comes in handy."

The idea of hibernation appealed to Pi. Unconsciousness on command.

"Monsieur, je m'appelle Pi."

"Enchantée, mon nom est, Pierre."

"Enchanté, monsieur Pierre."

"Excusez-moi mademoiselle. I'll be right back."

Pierre ducked beneath the surface and disappeared momentarily before resurfacing seconds later.

"Ah, that's better. Just needed to get a few bubbles of fresh water into my gills. Now, where were we? Ah yes, your name is Pi and my name is Pierre." He kept his head above the surface just enough so that he could see Pi with his dark eyes. His large tail buoyed his body in place. "Where are you headed mademoiselle?"

"North, to the sea."

"I see, I see." He dipped his head slightly so that trickles of water washed over his lower jaw and tongue. "That's quite a distance from here." He already knew the answer but asked, "Are you walking to the sea?"

"Oui."

"I see, I see." He spit a small fountain of water from his mouth. "Yes, I see, I see. And you have been walking for sometime now, non?"

"Oui."

"I see, I see."

"Well."

"Well....monsieur Pierre, I am very happy to see that you are well. Merci beaucoup for everything, I shall be on my way now."

"I'll take you to the sea."

"Excusez-moi?"

"I will take you to the sea. It doesn't matter which way I travel. Every direction is the same to me."

"But how do you propose to…"

"Get you there?"

"Yes."

"I already know how sharp your claws are, so if you stand on my back I'll swim you upstream."

"Have you done this before?"

"Non."

"Merci for your kind offer however, I think I'll continue walking."

"But if you travel with me you will save at least a day's journey. Now, I don't know how important a reason it is that you get to the sea, nor do I know how fast you need to get there but if you travel with me you'll get there in less than an hour."

Pi considered her options and saving an entire day's walk would bring her that much closer to finding Dr. Allbewell. "Monsieur Pierre? Do you mind if we try out, excusez-moi, a dry run?"

"That's a wonderful idea!" Pierre maneuvered himself closer to the bank of the river so that his body was parallel to the shore. "Okay, get on."

Pi slid down on his massive back and then latched on with

her claws.

"You can dig in a little deeper. You won't hurt me."

"Are you sure?"

"Yes, just a bit deeper, ahhhhhhh. Okay, that's deep enough."

"Je suis désolé."

"De rien. Ready?"

"Oui but please go slowly."

"Un, deux, trois!"

With a flick of his tail he began swimming up stream along the side of the riverbank, away from the strong currents. Pi held on tightly, her feet and tail sank below the surface creating a small, swirling wake behind. When her initial fear subsided she allowed a small smile to appear on her brave face. She lifted her head and stuck out her chest. The scene from the shore must have appeared quite surreal: a pigeon moving steadily up stream atop the river's surface. Her bright blue streak glistening and beaming in the afternoon sunlight, shining like a lighthouse beacon. With her wings tucked and her feet below the surface, she rode the river effortlessly with full and fixed eyes towards an unseen target, proud and confident.

"Monsieur Pierre?"

"Oui, Pi?"

"Merci beaucoup, mille fois merci."

"Are you comfortable enough for me to speed up a bit?"

"Oh yes. Yes I am. Full throttle please."

"Aye, aye captain."

Pierre's tail and fins propelled them quickly northward. Pi sat steadfast atop his back watching the countryside roll by in waves, moving faster than she ever could have imagined. *Maybe this is what flying feels like*, she mused.

A farmer on the river's right bank caught sight of the sailing bird and shouted to his son working the fields with him to look at the water bird but it was too late; she disappeared in a flash. The farmer's son shook his head and warned his father to get out of the hot sun.

"Merci, merci Pierre. I wish that we had met sooner!"

"Tout le plaisir était pour moi."

Pierre et Pi ils ont dansé la valse de l'eau à Saint-Just, Port-Mort, Courcelles-sur-Seine, autour du Le-Val-Saint-Martin, à Herqueville, Mesnil de Posses, autour d'Elbeuf, du via Le Clos Gosse, Ledu Hamel, de Saint-Adrien, viade Rouen et du Croisset et Le du coude de La Bouille, à la pointe de Berviille-sur-Seine via Le Conihout et Heurteauville et Villequier et Vieux-Port proche de l'embouchre de la Manche.

Upon reaching the gaping mouth of the English Channel, Pierre and Pi were sucked into its vastness, then tossed and swished, gargled and then coughed upward into a draft that carried them North East to the top of the cragged and chalked cliffs of Etretat.

The winds whipped their way up and over the backs of the cliffs causing tall grasses to sway and dance with wild mushrooms bobbing and rocking their heads to the beat.

Pi landed head first in a bowl of radiating yellow Genets. Carefree, they dipped and bowed their tiny wildflower pedals, giggling in the wind like children at a birthday party. Their tall stems yielded to the Norman winds with roots firmly planted in the silt loam.

Pi managed to pluck her head from the chalky soil and righted herself. The sun beamed and reflected the golden-colored flowers that were now embedded in her feathers, coating her from crown to tail. She looked around at the bustling seascape with sailboats and fishermen bobbing on the water and just above her head, several meters out from the cliffs, fantastical birds with large bodies, shiny heads and large, round eyes and wings stretched wider than she had ever seen before. They drifted effortlessly through the winds in enraptured delight. Gaining her balance, she walked down to the cliff's edge and scanned the slate grey waves that broke below in search for Pierre. Sculpted driftwood bobbed and tangled with bladderwrack seaweed. Together, they looked like a thin old man with long flowing green hair lazily drifting with the currents.

"Pierre? Pierre, where are you?" She looked east and west and out across the sea towards England with no sign of him. "Pierre? If you're here…Pierre?"

She backed away from the edge of the sea and sat down in the grass. A lump formed in her throat and she swallowed fighting back tears. *Pierre, oh wonderful Pierre…*she turned her head left then right and then behind her. A few meters away, wedged in a cluster of thorny milk thistle lay, Pierre. His body was covered in flesh-eating flies that feasted between his sharp scales. Fish netting wrapped his mouth, gills and fins.

"Pierre!!" She ran up the beach, almost flying to her friend. "Non, non, not Pierre. Please not Pierre!"

His left eye had locked its gaze on the sun confirming Pi's fears; milky and grey flies had feasted on it too. "Oh Pierre, I am so, so very sorry."

She sat stunned and mourned her loss. The flies, sun and wind slowly absorbed Pierre's body until the only things left were just a few shiny scales that pierced through the sharp thistle thorns. She watched the silvery scales sparkle and shimmer as a swarm of brown spotted mallow skipper butterflies swept over the tiny remains of the Great Sea Fish. Their paper-thin wings beat hundreds of graces that lifted and carried Pierre's soul far out into the Channel where it joined his mother, father and three siblings in a world where he would swim and jump and dive to his heart's content.

Pi wept for hours until the sun dropped behind the clouded horizon and the wind blew a soft whisper. Surely her beloved père no longer needed her help. *What's the point? I've cost Pierre his life; I've walked hundreds of miles…What was I thinking? Père is probably dead…what have I accomplished? Nothing.*

A gust of wind blew up the coast and the large winged birds with shiny heads looped and spiraled dangerously close to the cliffs. One, who had yellow and red striped wings, flew directly over Pi's head, its feet scraping her crown feathers. It caught a warm thermal and soared straight up into the sky through a powdered pink cloud. Pi followed it with her eyes looking to see where it would exit the cloud, and just when she thought it had disappeared, it swooped out from behind her. Its beak grabbed her between her legs and lifted her off the cliffs straight out over the Channel. She flew with the large winged bird high above the water gliding on gently rolling winds, sailing and soaring up and down through thin wisps of clouds until her natural instincts padded her with confidence. "Père! Look, I'm flying! I am flying!" The large winged bird climbed straight towards the sun and when it could fly no higher paused and pointed its nose down towards the Channel. Together, they sped through the air and when they were just several meters from the beach at Trouville-sur-Mer the bird lifted its beak, spread its great wings and slowly drifted to the pebbled beach, allowing Pi to gently slide from off its beak.

All was vacant on the beachfront, other than thousands of biting flies amassed at the breakwater. Their daily meeting was in session and their combined voices created a buzz that carried up and down the beach for miles.

In one cluster the argument was over direction. "I tell you, we should sweep north *then* south."

"Non, non, non. South *then* north."

"Mon Dieu! You are always wrong."

Another cluster, a bit larger and louder than the first, hungered for breakfast. "I don't give a rat's tail what or where we attack but I say damn it, let's get buzzing and eat something. It's time for petit déjeuner!"

"Oui, petit déjeuner!"

"Petit déjeuner! Petit déjeuner! Petit déjeuner! Petit

déjeuner!" They cried.

"Oui, I agree Louie. Let's get moving. Why the hell do we have to hover here every day anyway? We all want the same thing. We're just wasting good eating time. *Let's eats! Eats, eats, eats!*"

Others in the cluster joined him chanting, "*Eats, eats, eats, eats.*" In no time their mantra swept over the enormous cloud of hovering, buzzing and biting flies; cutting through les bras de mer and deep into the heart of any living creature within several miles. "Eats, eats, eats, eats," turned into one large cry, "Ezzzzzzzzzzzzzzzzz."

The sound driven by the wind swept into Pi's ears and grabbed her skull. "*Ohhhh, my....what is that...my head... arrêtez!!*"

En mass the flies were upon her stinging, biting, sucking, chewing. There was no escape from their relentless attack. One platoon drove themselves deep into her feathers burying razor-sharp teeth into her skin, ripping out small chunks of flesh while another detachment stung and bit her exposed eyes and ears. Bleeding, swelling, she ran to the safety of the Channel and immersed herself. The determined invaders clung to skin and feathers, refusing to yield to the cold and drowning waters. Their ferocity coupled with their numbers forced Pi to submerge herself repeatedly. Over and over she plunged trying to rid herself of her wretched oppressors. She held her breath as long as she could but they refused to let go. Struggling for air, she'd break the surface, inhale a gulp and then dive once again. Visions of the Paris sewer flowed through her brain. Over and over again she thrashed her body against the choppy waters until she was able to drain her tormentors of all their strength. One by one, exhausted and spent, they slowly and silently floated away in the murky water. Tiny, lifeless eyes like black pearls drifted aimlessly out into the darkness.

Pi shot to the surface gasping, filling her lungs. She panted heavily as blood pumped and flowed through her lungs and heart.

"Are they off? Are they off?!" She turned her head manically pecking at her back and tail feathers. "Get off, get off! You have eaten me through and through."

The flies were gone, washed away, but she felt their phantoms – their biting and gnawing felt real but were now imagined. Her head fell limp, the sand and pebbles beneath her feet slowly gave way, and she bobbed unconscious on her back as she drifted out to sea.

Chapter 11

HOURS ROLLED BY AND floated into days and nights as Pi drifted on the Sleeve. Noisy great black-backed gulls and kittiwakes flying overhead were not enough to rouse her. Neither were the intermittent lightning and thunderstorms that flashed and cracked. She dreamed, she floated, she dreamed.

Nhabellwoks. The Nhabellwoks will help you. Reach for them and they will take you home.

What are the Nhabellwoks?

It is not what little one, it is "who".

Pardon, who are the Nhabellwoks?

The Nhabellwoks will take you home. Call to them and they will answer. Call, "Nhabellwoks, Nhabellwoks." The voice was lilting and rang through the air with the clarity and directness of a great church bell. Pi tried moving her mouth to speak but her beak was crusted shut. She screamed without a voice that rang and reverberated only in her skull.

Call to them. Call, 'Nhabellwoks, please come and help me'.

I am calling but they cannot hear me!

Prisoner of her own body, tears delivered the only message that could be heard.

Do not cry child, I hear you. I will call the Nhabellwoks for you. They will come to your aid, they will save you from...I will call the

Nhabellwoks… Nhabellwoks…

The voice trailed off and sailed into a large, ash-gray colored cloud the shape of a horse.

Non, Pi cried. *S'il vous plaît do not leave me, s'il vous plaît I am calling, can't you hear me? Nhabellwoks, Nhabellwoks, Nhabell…*

The Sleeve turned and roiled and rolled itself, mixing and folding everything in its wake. Little birds awake and asleep were dragged and blended under the sea. Pipers and pigeons alike were churned and commingled until the Sleeve, satiated coughed and spit out the unwanted - the indigestible. Once again, Pi was shot from the sea - arced over the breakwaters and landed on long ago, discarded plastic bottles on the beach. And there she lay in cushioned waste far from the belly of the beast that flung her from its grip.

Pi? Pi, I'm here to help you.

Nhabellwoks? The Nhabellwoks are here. I can't see you, where are you Nhabellwoks?

This is your père. Who are the Nhabellwoks mon cher?

The Nhabellwoks' voices came to Pi through murk and haze, trauma and exhaustion, dehydration and hunger. The sea pushed her back to the shore where she struggled to open her eyes against the salt, sand and grunge that caked her face.

Riderless bicycles slept, perched on railings and rusted metal fences, looking like frozen and lost friends. Children's tattered kites with trails of twine crisscrossed the beach. Empty shells turned skyward, their tenants long ago departed for locations unknown.

"Where have I been? Señor Ernesto…? My head…I am so hungry…"

Her stomach churned with emptiness. In desperate need she slogged along the beach looking for a morsel, a slice, a piece of the smallest piece of pieces.

Feel. Feel beneath you.

"Who said that?…Hello?…'Feel beneath,' feel beneath what?"

Shifting her attention to the sand, she poked at it with her right foot and created a small pit. Water from the Channel slowly crept in and just beneath the surface a small round shell became visible. She seized it with her beak and then ran from the Channel's tides to a rock in the middle of the sandy beach. She watched as a brown and rubbery body wriggled its head through a chink in the shell. She stood staring at the creature between her feet. *I'm so hungry...but I can't...I can't eat another... But I must eat...How do I know that it wasn't put here in this spot just so that I might find it? Should I ignore such a gift?*

The creature in the shell stopped writhing and gave itself to rest in Pi's claws.

"Oh non. Oh non, non, non. I've killed it! I killed it." She stared at the lifeless creature at her feet not knowing what to do. I should give it back. But her hunger had a different answer: *Eat it now. It's no good to anyone else now. You're hungry, so it eat before you're dead too.*

She debated over and over. She thought about her own life and dying on the beach. Would she slowly stop moving and molt and melt into the sand? *I have to eat. I must eat. It's necessary. I need to get to...and get back to père and mère.* She closed her eyes and squeezed the shell tightly, put the head of the rubbery body in her beak and bit down hard. She held it in her mouth and winced from the strange texture. *I can't do it. I simply can't do it.* She spat the piece of flesh into the sand and collapsed.

Eat it. The voice commanded again.

"I can't. I've tried. I just can't do it."

You must. Other's lives depend upon it.

"Je suis folle. I must be going crazy."

Trust. Eat the meat.

Once again she put the rubbery morsel of meat on her tongue and held it there. This time the salty taste and texture felt familiar. She held her breath, closed her eyes and swallowed. Her face contorted as the food slid down her throat and into her belly. She opened her eyes and waited. Instant nourishment was sent out from the center of her belly to the rest of her body. Hungry for more, she rushed to the breakwater to unearth new shells. She dug with both feet and mined les riches de mer. Bushels of snails sprouted from their wet and sandy homes and became caught between her claws. No sooner had she pecked the meat from one shell, ten more rose to the surface. It was an endless culinary crustacean feast with no end to the flow. She pecked and ate and ate and pecked. With each swallow her belly expanded. Big and bloated she bit and swallowed more than she could hold until she came to an abrupt stop.

The voice interrupted, *Arrêtez! You've had enough.* Pi heeded, but only for a moment. She stared straight out across the Channel, her eyes glazed with obsession. Once again, she plunged her face into the sand like a steam shovel hauling meters of earth in one gulp. The shells spilled out of the corners of her hinged mouth as she took on bigger payloads than she could hold. Lost in her consumption she no longer took the time to remove the meat from the spiral shaped shells; she swallowed them whole. And then it happened. The walls of her stomach reached their breaking point. They could expand no more and then ruptured. The earth began to spin and the beach wobbled and rocked like a hobbyhorse. Her eyes swirled counter to the rhythm of the spinning earth as voluminous fumes and gases percolated deep in her bowels. Like a volcano, the gases gathered heat, steam and fire and slowly rose filling every available hollow in her tiny body. Out of her gluttonous rampage she ballooned; her shape stretched to its capacity. Her feet, head and even her feathers expanded to grotesque proportions. She became so inflated that her eyes vanished into her swollen face.

Like the storm brewing on her insides the weather on sur la Marche grew blustery. Wind and tide whipped the waters of the Channel into choppy whitecaps while ragtag gangs of sandstorms snapped and lashed at anything standing in their path. With her eyes plugged hopelessly into her face, she stumbled aimlessly about the beach trying to gain her bearings.

The winds now at gale force swept up the sand, grabbed Pi under her wings, picked her up and tossed her down the beach like feathered tumbleweeds. Head over tail across the beach, over and over she was blown until she was slammed into a large trunk of driftwood wedged in the sand. Filled with noxious gases, she was lifted off the beach, carried upward and hurdled west. Carried higher and higher, flying without the use of her wings, unable to see ahead or below, she sailed along blind. Up and up, into the troposphere, away from terra firma drifting like a wayward helium balloon with no compass, without direction. Cumulous clouds parted and tore like thinly woven cotton. The sun pierced the turquoise colored water below. Seagulls gliding on thermals caught sight of Pi sailing aimlessly beneath their gleaming white bodies then dove towards her for a closer look.

Pi lost consciousness. The seagulls ascended and pecked at her rump, head and wings. Blood oozed from the roots of her quills and formed into tiny red droplets that trickled to the chilly waters below. The droplets floated briefly on the surface before being enveloped into the trillions of gallons of water.

The gulls' assaults continued over and over and the hunter became the hunted. The droplets of blood gushed and trailed to the sea like a liquid kite ribbon. Life hemorrhaged with each peck from the gulls' sharp and pointed beaks. They tore deeper and deeper into her flesh. And then in an instant, they disengaged, pulled up and away from their prey, as if answering an unheard command. They arched their necks, pointed their heads and ascended northward.

The heavens unfurled a ribbon of warm air that slipped under Pi and cradled her like a broad soft hand. It swayed her gently back and forth and deposited her in the soft sand. Depleted of blood, food and energy she lay on the deserted beach with nothing but the dry sand. She slept for hours and hours with endless dreams, through violent hailstorms and winds swept with salt, sand, stones and splinters of driftwood. All through the night until the next morning when the day's light turned orange and the Channel dark gray, she dreamt.

In the broad light of the rising sun a lone young, female gull walked along the shore. She pecked and sang at the churning surf in search of her morning meal. Her feathers, blinding white, made a beautiful contrast to the red tuft of feathers that sat atop her crown.

"Je ni'a pas de regret. I have nooooooo regrets, no regrets. But should I have regrets…hmmm, hmmm, hmmm. Je ni'a pas de regret… What have we here?" Stumbling upon Pi's place of respite, the gull inspected her with caution. She encircled several times then gently poked her with her long white beak. Pi screeched with fear recognizing the invader as a gull.

"Oh, I'm so sorry, I didn't mean to frighten you."

Pi looked down at her still oozing wounds and became light headed.

"Mercy, you got into a fight didn't you?"

"Non, I was not in a fight. I ate something that did not fully agree with me and then I was attacked by a pack of hungry and vicious gulls that looked a lot like you."

"I know that song mademoiselle. Many times I shouldn't have eaten something because I knew that it would me make me sick but I had no power to say no to it and before I knew it, I ate it and then I'm praying to the heavens again for relief." She flipped her head around her shoulders and returned it to face Pi. "What vicious gulls?! Non, non, non, non. We are not vicious. Hungry yes but vicious non. Pardon my being so coarse.

My name is Louise."

"Enchanté. Je m'appelle, Pi. Mademoiselle, these gulls who did this to me were cruel and inflicted these wounds with precision, so much so that I cannot remember the entire ordeal; I fainted rather quickly."

Louise let out a laugh that squeezed through her nose, which sounded like a high-pitched boat horn.

"I am glad that you find my being attacked so humorous."

"I am truly sorry, I didn't mean to..." She couldn't help herself and again cackled with laughter. "Oh, I am so sorry; sometimes I have no control. I just started doing it one day when I was very depressed. I tried everything else and found that I became so happy, so I thought why not continue laughing all the time?"

Louise's depression stemmed from the loss of her brother to a tragic accident ten years ago during a family outing to the Outer Hebrides. Her brother Aralt was lean and strong with purpose-filled grey eyes and seven years from the hatch, when the family lifted off for the Scottish Islands. It was Aralt who led the family across the Channel playfully and competitively jockeying for point position with his father. It was Aralt who first spotted their cousins the Abernothenoths' as they waved from the Scottish machair. Louise, three years' Aralt's junior, tried to keep up with her swift brother when he made like a rocket to the sand dunes below. He probably never heard her cry "wait for me!" as he descended with the anticipation of seeing his cousins and listening to their fantastical yarns.

He died painlessly, is what Louise tells herself everyday. *A freak accident. Something that only happens once in a hundred years...*

As Aralt approached the Scottish dunes he made an "L" shaped turn and cruised over cresting waves, when from out of nowhere a massive hulk of tongue, teeth and muscle breached the water and snatched Aralt into its gaping mouth, just as he shouted "bonjour" to his cousin Fingal.

No one on the beach moved. Everything and everyone froze. Louise and her family who witnessed the horrific sight from above stopped mid-air, petrified. Louise dropped from the sky with wings tucked and dove into the cold and infested waters and searched for her brother. Her parents' screams to stop went unheeded as Louise was below the surface in a matter of seconds. When she resurfaced, she clutched her brother's only remains: a battered slate gray colored feather in her beak.

"Is there anything that I can do for you?"

"Unless you're able to fly me across the Channel..." Pi paused and retracted her sarcasm, "Merci, non there is nothing. Thank you for asking."

"You can't fly?"

"Non."

"I see."

"Do you?"

"I'm sorry, I don't mean to stare it's just that..."

"That you have never come across a bird that cannot fly?"

"Well, yes."

"Now that you have, what do you think?"

"Well I certainly couldn't tell by just looking at you. You appear to be normal. Although, you do have an interesting blue streak running through your breast feathers." She stepped behind Pi and inspected her tail feathers. "Everything seems to be in order. Is it some sort of birth defect or something?"

"Mademoiselle, if we had more time perhaps, we would have the opportunity to discuss this subject in detail but I must be moving on."

"What's across the Channel?"

"Que?"

"I mean, why do you need to get across the Channel and how can you if you can't fly?"

"As I said, there's no time to explain."

"Well, pardonez-moi. Excuse me for being interested. As a matter of fact, excuse me for *being!*"

"I'm sorry but I have been traveling for a very long time and I just don't have the time to…"

"Forget it. I don't want to know."

Pi took a deep breath. "Louise is it?" Louise gave a nonchalant bob of her head. "Louise, je suis désolé. My father is… he might already be…I have to get to England that's all. Now, I must be leaving you."

Louise turned ever so slightly to face Pi and bowed her head with a bit of shame. "Mademoiselle, I am truly sorry. Had you told me this before I would have stopped chattering away hours ago."

A small gust of wind stirred around their feet and created an invisible lasso.

"We'll fly you there!"

"That's not possible, you know that."

"C'est vrai, unless we make you something to fly in."

"I don't understand."

"Écoutez. I can fly right?"

"Oui."

"All we have to do is make something that you can sit in and I can pull it until you get airborne. It's brilliant! Just brilliant." She sent out a laugh that sailed across the Channel, bounced off the English cliffs and smacked her back in the face.

"Louise, I thank you for your good intentions but it sounds dangerous, time consuming, and I just don't have anymore time to spare. I shall stay with my present mode of transportation, which has been reliable and has brought me this far."

"Mademoiselle Pi, you yourself said that you have no time to spare, so why waste more time walking when you can fly?"

"I love the idea of flying; however, I gave up on flight a long time ago. If you would like to walk with me for a bit, I would welcome the company."

"Pi, give me two hours to come up some sort of contraption for you to fly in and if, after that time we can't make it work then you can start walking again. What do you say?"

She mulled the idea over with the thought of crossing the wide expanse of the Channel and then agreed. "I don't like the sound of "contraption" but okay, two hours and two hours only."

Louise didn't quite have a formal plan for her flying machine but she was determined. From a distance she thought that she had once seen the carrion of a herring gull being carried across the horizon on a flat bed of various woven materials. It was towed oddly enough by a yellow-legged gull.

"Start looking for some of that...what's it called? Hmm, weed? Seaweed? Yes, that's it! I believe that its correct name is wakame."

"I'm impressed." Pi said. "Where did you learn that?"

"My brother..." She stopped mid-sentence and dropped her head. She could still taste his wet and wilted feather in her mouth.

"Louise, what is it?"

"It's nothing. Let's advance."

"What am I looking for Louise?"

"I'm not sure but I'll know it when I see it."

The tide was moving in along the coast bringing with it debris from last night's storm: plastic yokes, rotted timber, colored cloth, resin pellets and various items of discarded garbage.

"There! Look at that, that's a start." Louise pointed to a small soup can with a tattered label. "There's your cockpit."

"My what?"

"Your cockpit, where you'll sit while I pull."

"Louise, I don't..."

"We only have two hours. The more questions you ask the longer it will take for you to get across the Channel."

They pecked, pulled, carried, and pushed strands of sailor's rope, discarded scraps of clothing, shredded rubber tires, abandoned parts of plastic toys and miscellaneous flotsam and jetsam. The carelessness of others provided the necessary materials for the makeshift-flying contraption. Within an hour they had everything they needed to start construction, and with time to spare it was completed and ready for testing.

"Alright, get in," Louise instructed.

"Are you sure about this?"

"Come on, get in so we can try it."

Hesitantly, Pi reared herself into the rusty soup can. Her head and tail feathers spilled over the rim, her breast pressed tightly against the sides, staining her blue streak rusty orange.

"Comfy?"

"Not really. It's rather tight in here."

"Stand taller and you'll be skinnier."

"Que?"

The soup can sat in a basket made up of threads of sailor's rope, which had two long strands. The two strands came together six feet away from the can and were bound together by more of the same. Louise hopped over to the bounded ends of rope and slipped them in her beak like a horse bit. Speaking through a tightly closed mouth she muttered, "Okay, get ready for takeoff."

"Would you please repeat that, I did not hear you?"

Louise dropped the bit. "I said, get ready for takeoff."

Pi braced herself and prayed, "Mon Dieu! Save us all."

With the bit back in her beak, Louise walked forward taking up slack in the rope until it was stretched tight. Slivers of fiber split from the rope and floated away into the sea air. The soup can lurched forward from the tension put upon it. Louise dug her heels into the sand and flapped her wings causing Pi and the can to lurch further forward.

"Arrettez! Louise! Stop. I'm falling…" Louise, who couldn't hear Pi's protestations, beat her wings, which hurled sand into the air. The combined weight of Pi and the soup can played tug-of-war with her attempts to get airborne. She beat her wings harder and harder until slowly she lifted from the sand. As Louise ascended, Pi dropped back into the can, its rusty bottom scraping on sand and pebbles. Finally, Louise, Pi and the soup can pushed through gravity and sailed up the beach.

"We're flying! We're actually flying. I told you it would work!"

Pi opened her eyes and peered over the rim and smiled, as she was actually airborne. At last, even though just a passenger, the joy of flight filled her with excitement and she took delight tilting her head towards the heavens. "Père, I'm flying, I'm flying! Are you proud Papa? C'est fantastique!"

"How are you doing back there?"

"Parfait! Wonderful. I never knew flying could be so marvelous."

Tailwinds crept up on Louise and eased her efforts and propelled them faster through the afternoon skies. "Ah, that's more like it. Winds on the old tail."

They sailed along covering a lot of ground until the skies turned grey and the temperature plummeted. The cold air stung, and Pi inflated herself, bulging the sides of the soup can in order to conserve body heat.

"Louise, the weather doesn't look promising. Maybe we should stop."

"Non. The weather is the weather as it always is. It will change quickly."

This was of no comfort to Pi and the skies agreed with her as they instantaneously erupted and shot spikes of frozen rain in every direction. A sharp pointed piece thrown with the precision of an expert's knife stabbed Louise in the center of her right eye sending cold, steel pain to every nerve. She froze mid-flight then paused before her brain recognized the frozen blade in her head. She dropped out of the air like a sack of rocks that pulled Pi down with her to the rocky shore.

Pi wrenched herself from the can and walked towards Louise who was splayed and tangled in ropes a few meters down the beach.

"Louise? Louise, are you alright?" There was no movement and Pi nudged her head. "Louise, please...This can't be happening, not here, not now."

Louise's left leg was broken in two places. Part of it was behind her back lying under her dead weight.

"Oh non. Oh non, Louise, please wake up." She looked around for help but the beach was abandoned. "Louise, you have to get up. I can't...I have to...I can't...I just can't."

She rushed to the Channel's edge and gulped as much water has she could hold in her mouth then sprayed it on Louise's head. It aroused her instantly, "What happened?"

"Merci, mon Dieu."

"We were flying then we took a nose dive and I...how did my foot get behind my....*Yaaaageeeeeeeee!!*"

Upon seeing her leg bent in two, Louise again fell unconscious. Pi rushed back down to the Channel and brought more water to spit on Louise's face. It had no effect. She ran down and back again and again until on her last attempt Louise awoke.

Wet and cold with a broken leg, Louise sobbed, "Pi, go on without me. There's no hope for me here. I'll be someone else's dinner tonight and you need to march on."

"I'm not leaving you Louise. I'll find help and be back before dark."

"Pi, please go. I got us into this mess. It's not fair for you to be kept here. Your father needs you. Please, go."

"Non! Ce n'est pas possible. You will die from the cold." She scanned the beach for shelter and noticed a narrow tunnel of some sort in the distance. "Voila! La! I'll take you over there and you'll at least have some protection from the wind and rain until I can get some help."

"I can't move my leg Pi. How do you suppose that I get there?"

"You carried me and now I will carry you. My legs are stronger than most. I will get you into the can and then pull you."

It was a huge effort but Pi managed to get Louise into the soup can and pulled her with the already knotted ropes to an abandoned drainage pipe ten meters down the beach.

"You'll be safe in here until I can get help," Pi's voiced echoed. "I'll be back as soon as I can. Try not to move too much."

"Pi, don't come back for me. Just go, I'll be alright."

They looked at each other knowing that wasn't true. Pi bent down and kissed Louise on the top of her head. "I will be back for you, and if you don't see me soon someone will come for you. I will send someone for you. I will not leave you to die here Louise, I will not."

"I know you won't. I look forward to seeing you again someday soon. Au revoir."

"Au revoir mon amie."

Don't look back, don't look back, Pi told herself as she walked away. It was all she could do to keep her head and eyes fixed on her own two feet. Not until the sun was low in the sky and everything on the beach was blanketed in muted light did she dare to turn her head. The distance was too great, too far for even her eyes to make out a shape now so small on the landscape. After walking for hours without passing another soul, she stopped and said, "Bon chance Louise. Bon chance."

Chapter 12

FROM WHERE PI LEFT Louise to her present location had taken her through gravel and pitted roads. Mud, soot and spray had caked down to the roots of her quills. Her heels, cracked and bloodied, left her with a severe limp.

The hours passed slowly as did the miles. The late afternoon sun slipped in and out of white, gray and pink clouds. When the quarter moon had risen, Pi ended her search for a place to sleep. An abandoned sand snake barrow would provide what she needed. Once ensconced, she tried to lull herself to sleep with a song her father used to sing to her when she was a young squab.

> *Mon enfant, mon enfant, c'est vrai la terre est ronde*
> *Et longtemps, j'ai cherché l'oiseau bleu dans le monde*
> *Comme toi, j'ai pleuré en tendant mes deux bras*
> *Mais pour toi, j'en suis sûre un beau jour il viendra*

A consistent scratching and drilling beneath the barrow's floor kept her awake no matter what song she hummed to herself. And when she did finally fall asleep, the noise and vibrations emanating from beneath her crept into every frame of her dreams.

Red ants oozed into her dreams. One by one they walked the catwalks of her brain and out onto the planks that crossed thousands of deep crevices filled with electrical impulses and black tissue. These imps of the night ascended spiral staircases and upon reaching the uppermost step, paused and looked out onto a valley of jumping and twitching ideas, thoughts, musings, rationalizations, tenets, morals, and inspirations. They quickly pushed forward as the traffic flow continued on in a steady pace up the stairs until each one plunged into the depths below where they floundered and splashed in a sea of sand and uncertainty. They never stopped their ascent up the stairs and their flow down the chutes to earth and sand. They gasped at the task at hand only to start the journey all over again. This cycle continued over and over unabated and without relief all in an effort to construct the greatest fortress that had ever been built so that she could not rest.

At daybreak, Pi rose and started to run westward. Slowly at first then faster and faster until her lungs filled to capacity. "I'm running, I'm running! Look at me, I'm running!" And she did, she ran as fast as she could with the wind at her back. The sand whipped behind her as her feet kicked over and over. *Fast, fast, very fast.* The sensation was liberating and she was overcome with joy and renewed energy. *Fast, faster, faster.* Faster, until she was stopped in her tracks by a sea of golden genets. They held her in their embrace like a loving friend, comforting, enveloping, and swaying her in their long and winding arms of green. Their yellow pear and bell shaped flower faces caressed and tickled her until she giggled and laughed and then she couldn't stop. It felt too good, and she laughed with her complete soul and with every ounce of breath in her lungs. When the genets felt it time, they lifted their faces to the turquoise painted sky and blew puffs of powdery grains no bigger than a spec of a whit, that showered down on Pi like a soft rain, that wrapped her in a blanket of gold, and then and only then did they release their loving embrace.

Chapter 13

Forty miles north at Courseulles-sur-Mer a flock of fifty gathered atop the roof of a weathered barn with the morning sun warming their faces. The eldest, a male pigeon of great respect and knowledge known only as Achelles, sat with claws locked into the rotted shingles, recounting the celebrated tale of the Magnificent Golden Bird of Brittany. The Golden Bird had not been seen in hundreds of years but that didn't stop anyone from believing.

On the yearly anniversary of the Magnificent Golden Bird's arrival, the youngest of the flock gathered tightly around Achelles' feet with rapturous eyes and clung to his every word. No matter that the flock's elders had heard this tale every year since they could first understand words, they too stood with rapt attention and with the hope that *today* would be the day that the Magnificent Golden Bird of Brittany appeared.

The revered old bird addressed his audience; "It was on the ninth day of June in the year of the Aigle that a immense crowd descended upon the muddy, shallow waters. All the great birds were there: Aurora, Quirinos, Corentin, and Célestin. They alighted upon the gathered crowd as gracefully and delicately as les Bouton d'or. Monsieur Tournachon, the great, great, grandson of the anointed monsieur Richel Tournachon gasped when he felt a wave of the infinite splash through his chest. He knew that something spectacular was about to take place."

One of the squeakers just learning to speak whispered to his mother, "Mère, what does in-fly-night mean?" His mother covered her young squab's head with her wing in embarrassment. No one dared interrupt Achelles during his storytelling; it could result in banishment.

Achelles liked to tell his stories with great flair; to interrupt him would cost him vast amounts of intellectual energy. So much so that he would have to reschedule his storytelling for another day. "Je suis dégoûté!" he declared the first and only time he was forced to abort his story. A small riot ensued.

"We left our homes and went like lemmings all at once, as if being called by the Master Conductor." He bowed his head so that his eyes met his audiences'. "The ignorant believe that we have a homing device, or something to that extent, but it is our high level of intuitiveness that gives us our sense of direction and we just go to where it is that we are supposed to be."

Without thinking a young male with checkered wings shouted out, "Monsieur Achelles!" A gasp arose from the crowd as they looked to the checkered bird then to Achelles.

"Pardon Monsieur, s'il vous plaît. What happened next?"

Achelles' claws curled under his feet and he grew an inch taller. The veins in his forehead began to bulge along with his chest. The crowd held their breath as he lifted his wings and aimed daggers at the young bird and shot his question dead to the ground. The young bird bowed his head with embarrassment and slowly, like a deflating balloon, Achelles unfurled his claws. No one dared move, as they waited for Achelles to say or do something.

"We knew that we had come that day for a reason, although, we did not know what the reason was until much later."

He took a dramatic pause and then said, "The Channel waters were restless and irritable and the waves crested, crashed and then clapped like giant wings. The skies grew dark until only a small slit oozed greenish-blue light. Nothing stirred on the beach. No crabs, no insects, nothing. Everyone was buried deep in their homes or fled the area completely. Le temps était… how should I say…" Achelles rocked back and forth on his gray little feet looking for the right balance of words. "Ah, bon! The weather was dangereuse. Its face looked like that of a bird gone *fou*. So insane that the little slit in the sky rolled and formed into two ovals shaped like eyes and through the eyes came a…" He stopped mid-sentence, held his breath and scanned his audience. The squab's faces held a gaping beak. Their bodies lurched forward in anticipation. He continued, "The dark clouds folded into themselves and vanished and the eyes of the slit in the sky opened, pouring out golden light from the heavens. The entire sea was bathed in warm and peaceful light. A blanket of absolute tranquility lay over everything. All became completely still."

Achelles steeped in memory said not another word for what seemed an eternity. Drool seeped from the corner of his beak and the young birds at his feet stared not knowing whether to laugh or fly away in fear. A midge buzzed by his ear waking him from his daydream. He took a moment to survey himself and his strange deportment and then gathered his confidence with a swift lifted wing that stretched out over his audience. "And then from over the cliffs came the faint sound of music being played, and in unison we turned and faced where it was coming from. It was the strangest and most beautiful sound that I have ever heard." He took a deep breath in and puffed out his chest. His audience saw reflected in his eyes the image of what came over that cliff top so many years ago. "Mon Dieu, it was spectacular! A golden orb crested the cliff filling the land with golden light as far as the eye could see. It was brighter than the core of the sun and we shielded our eyes from the searing light." Several of the young birds at Achelles' feet squinted their eyes and buried their heads in the feathers of their chests.

"After our eyes adjusted to the grand soleil we could see the outline of a bird, a bird just like you and me except that the orb-like bird was big. Very big. As tall and as wide as the barn that we are perched on." Achelles stretched his wings out as far as they would go casting a shadow across the first few rows of the entranced flock.

"Mère," one of the young peepers called to his mother. "I want to go home." His mother held him close and assured him that every peeper and squeaker for hundreds of years had heard the tale of the Magnificent Golden Bird of Brittany and that they all lived to tell about it.

Achelles had his audience in the crook of his claw and wasted no time in bringing them to the peak of his story. "Mesdames, messieurs, et les enfants. It is was at this point that the Magnificent Golden Bird stood at the precipice of the chalky cliff and began to flap her enormous wings, lifting the heads of creeping buttercups, pearlworts and globe thistles, tearing them from their stems and sending them sailing into the Norman winds. And then it rained. The buttercups, pearlworts and thistles showered down on us in big, soft and sloppy drops of yellow, purple, and fuchsia and as we bathed in the warm colors of the flowers the Magnificent Golden Bird beamed a smile and said, 'Ma cher famille. Votre maison est l'endroit le plus beau sur la terre. Yes, she called our home the most beautiful place on earth and she went on to say, 'Vous serez jeune pour toujours. Vous avez été choisie!'"

Achelles' eyes welled with tears; something that no one in the flock had ever seen before. Scabious flower hairs floated in the air and scraped the heads of the tall males standing at the back of the crowd. The flock was completely hushed until a school of dolphins fifty meters out in the Channel leaped and whistled. Once again Achelles was brought out of his stupor and bowed his head forcefully and attempted to disguise his waning bravado. He cleared his throat, switched his weight from his left leg to the right and addressed the children softly, "Mes enfants doux des cieux, my dear sweet children of the skies, the Magnificent Golden Bird lifted from the top of the cliff and hovered for a moment and said, 'Buvez, chers amis! Buvez les couleurs pour la jeunesse éternelle. Drink; drink the colors for eternal youth,' she directed and then flew out across the Channel towards Brittany."

"What about the colors?" Someone daringly shouted from the back of the flock.

"Ah yes, les couleurs. The buttercups, pearlworts, and thistles and all the others that laid everywhere, softened and melted into rainbow-colored puddles and the puddles collected themselves and turned into a cool lake that crept up our legs to the crest of our chests. We stood mesmerized in watercolors; transfixed, frozen in time."

Achelles dropped his pretensions and airs, looked into the peach-tinted eyes of an innocent looking squab and said, "And do you know what happened next?" Without waiting for an answer he looked North and threw his words out to the Channel, "Buvez…buvez mes amis. Buvez." His words drifted out over the water and then back to the flock like a boomerang. "And we did. We bowed our heads to the rainbow-colored lake and sucked up the cool water and as it slid down our throats the heart of the sun opened in our stomachs and radiated out to the tips of every feather."

Like a connoisseur, Achelles drew in a deep breath of saltwater air and let it swirl around his nostrils. An astonished young, rusty-red bird opened his beak wide to ask a question but nothing came out. Achelles knew what he was going to ask, the same question that is asked every year when he tells the story of the Golden Bird. "Oui, c'est vrai. Myself and all the elders of our great flock are as old, or I should say, are as young as the day the Great Golden Bird of Brittany came to us hundreds of years ago."

The children were astonished. They looked at each other in disbelief not knowing if their little brains were playing tricks on them. Turning to their elders they weighed them from tip to tail searching for any signs of age, but there were none to be found. With a nod, the elders smiled knowingly and guided the young ones back to Achelles.

"C'est vrai, c'est vrai," Achelles repeated. "We have waited as your brothers, sisters and cousins have waited for hundreds of years for the Golden Bird to return and shower us with her Golden Light, colored wildflowers and cool waters of eternal youth. But alas, it appears not to be." The squabs, peepers and squeakers brimmed questions from every pore and ascended upon Achelles en masse. "Children, children I must leave you now."

Every year, just prior to telling the story of the Golden Bird and immediately after, Achelles felt weak and old. It was as if *he* was starting to age, and maybe for the first time since that Golden Bird alighted on the cliffs, the miracle was fading.

A newfound respect grew for the old master. Perhaps unknowingly, the children of the flock began to revere him for who he was not what he was. This is what he quietly longed for. He walked slowly to the south corner of the barn roof. The flock opened a path for him as he sidestepped gouges in the shingles. At the tip of the pitched roof he hopped up onto a tarnished brass finial and surveyed his land. *For thousands of years we have flown above this beautiful countryside. Peacefully and gracefully we have lived, wed, birthed and…* The thought hit him like an arrow in the head. For him the cycle will never be completed. This is what had plagued him for the last year or so. He had thought that his sadness was because he felt there was so much more to do with his life; places to see, friends to fly with.

"Monsieur Achelles!" One of the squeakers shouted. "Look there on the cliff."

A golden hue pulsated from the tall grass. Warmth radiated from deep within while gnats sleeping in their leafy beds spat out in all directions creating a curtained pathway. Achelles' feathered ends piqued and stood at attention. His heart pounded in anticipation. *Could it be? Has she come back to fill the shores with colors and to reverse the cycle?* His thoughts raced ahead as the glow grew brighter and the heat intensified. The flock gasped, as the grasses parted and golden light flashed across their faces. Each and every bird stood frozen and hypnotized.

I cannot believe it! She has returned. She has returned! Achelles tried to fly to the Golden Bird but could not manage to get his wings to move.

Making her way to the base of the barn the golden bird looked up to the flock on the roof and said, "Bon jour. It is so very good to see you. I have been traveling for a very long time without seeing or speaking to anyone."

Covered with the golden petals and pollen of the genets flowers, there wasn't a sign of the blue streak running down Pi's chest or a hint of a gray feather to be seen.

"Your Greatness?!" Achelles shouted with childlike excitement. "I am…we are so humbled by your appearance."

"Pardon?"

"Excuse me your Greatness, where are my manners?" He directed his attention to his flock and commanded, "Attention! Greeting formation, maintenant!"

In synchronized formation the flock alighted, tucked their legs under their bodies and lowered their beaks to the ground. Their tails splayed across each other's creating one large fanned tapestry of feathers.

"Your Greatness, je suis Achelles. My flock and I welcome you. We bow to you and all that you are. Please, walk and trample across our backs as a sign and demonstration of our humbleness and your Greatness."

Pi looked across the wave of prostrated bodies and back

to Achelles and wondered who he thought she was. "Monsieur Achelles, I believe that you are mistaken. I am not, I assure you, not considered 'great' by anyone."

With a raised eyebrow Achelles addressed the flock. "Do you hear friends? The humblest of the humble shows you her Greatness by refusing to be put on a pedestal where she belongs." Turning back to Pi he smiled and in a lowered voice continued, "But of course, mademoiselle, whatever title you prefer we defer and will refer to you as would be our honor and privilege."

"Monsieur Achelles, s'il vous plaît.. Ask your flock to please stand. I am no one of importance. I assure you that you are mistaken."

"Whatever you wish your Greatness." He turned to the flock where a single peeper stuck his head out of the crowd to catch a glimpse of the Golden Bird. Achelles raised and spread his wings and then commanded, "Flock. Levez-vous!" The flock rose to their feet in one single motion creating a loud *floghloissshhh*. "You see your Greatness, your every desire is our command. Now, how can I please you? What is that I can get for you? Anything, anything at all that you desire we will get for you."

"That is very kind of you monsieur Achelles but again, I am not who you think I am."

"Who is anyone? What are we? Where have we come from? Where are we going? Where are we now? Yes, yes, yes, these are life's timeless questions and I suspect, that as a lesson to us all, you will not be giving us the answers."

"If only I had the answers myself, I would surely share them with you."

"I have just one request your Greatness and that is for you to end this endless cycle that I have been on. I realize that we are all teachers and I have given much to my students but it is time for me to move on, is it not?"

"Monsieur Achelles, I wish that I could honor your request

but I have not one jot of power to grant it."

His face fell. His head followed and drooped to his chest. Through his feathers he said, "Ah, but of course, it is not solely within your power I suppose. Others must be consulted. Heavenly congresses to be convened."

"Yes, something of that nature."

"Would you, beautiful, Golden One, please take my request when you leave and submit it to the Powers that be? Will you also kindly be certain that this wonderful flock that you see before you is always watched over and cared for, protected and loved?"

"Well, I…I will tell whoever I meet of your concerns and they will tell others and the Greatest of Birds will watch over you and your flock."

The Master Conductor was finally ready to let go of his baton. Until now he had not showed so much emotion. Burying his face in Pi's breast feathers he wept like a motherless squab. His tears seeped through the layer of golden powdery grain covering Pi's feathers and grew into a golden stream that flowed and pooled at their feet. Her goldenness gone, the crowd gasped and flew in each and every direction. Devastated, Achelles lost consciousness and dropped to the ground. With a sense of amusement Pi chuckled, "This cannot possibly be happening." She tried to wake him with the tip of her right wing. "Monsieur Achelles…" She turned out towards the Channel looking for a member of the flock. "If there is a Great Golden Bird, now would be a very good time to appear and lend a wing." A slip of waxed paper wrapped itself around her legs and snapped in the wind. She stood there with the paper rapping at her knees, the Channel's waves crashing in the distance. A male blind ringlet butterfly alighted on Pi's head, his brown and burnt orange colored wings beat gently against her crown feathers. With antennas glistened in the setting sun and his eyes set north, he spoke through the furry underside of his body, "They won't be coming back until you leave."

Pi hadn't noticed that the Ringlet landed on her head, "Who said that?"

"Atop your head my friend."

She flipped her eyes upward to see only its translucent antennas. "What are you doing up there?"

"Everyone has to be somewhere so why not here? Besides, I was sent to give you directions?"

"Sent? Sent by whom?"

"The one with the directions."

"Come down where I can see you please."

"Non."

"Non?"

"Oui, non."

"If I can't see you I can't trust you."

"Must you see to trust?"

"Yes."

"Why?"

Pi reached for an answer but couldn't find one that she'd be willing to share with the stranger. "Well, I'm not sure but if I could see your face then I would know if you were telling me the truth."

"Hmm, I find that line of thinking so pedestrian, so primitive, so boring, and unfortunately, so predictable."

"Pardonnez-moi?"

"Why, oh why is it so de rigueur for you and so many others to believe with only your narrow minds?

"Monsieur, you are absolutely being…"

"You're wasting precious time arguing. If you don't want the information that I have for you then I shall leave."

"I didn't say that."

"Bon. Proceed on your course northwest until you come upon an egret with white hair."

Pi interrupted, "A what?"

"An egret with white hair."

"What is an egret?"

"I have no idea but you will know it when you stumble upon it."

"That's it? That's all the information that you have for me?"

"Oui mademoiselle."

"Well, what am I to do with it?"

"Start walking."

"Yes, I suppose…wait a moment. How did you know that I…?"

"Can't fly?"

"Oui."

"We blind ringlets hear everything. Things that you sighted folks could never imagine. You miss seeing so much every day because you can't hear."

"Mes oreilles work perfectly."

"And therein lies the problem."

"What are you talking about Monsieur?"

"That is all I have to say on the subject mademoiselle. Bon voyage."

As lightly and undetected as he landed, his weightless legs pushed off from the crown of Pi's head. He fluttered away, his colors blended with the surrounding thistles, genets and tall grasses. And as he disappeared a faint, "Bon chance," slipped through the folds in the wind.

Pi tried in vain to arouse Achelles. His flock was nowhere to be seen. "Monsieur Achelles? Monsieur?" The pools of colors at her feet slowly turned grey. "I am so sorry that I am not, could not be the golden bird that you needed me to be."

Chapter 14

AFTER THREE DAYS AND forty miles, Pi had given in to exhaustion. She buried herself beneath a cold top layer of beach sand then fell into a deep sleep.

The great waters of the Channel were restless. It laughed and snickered and tempted one with an invitation to come closer, to dip their feet. When they did, a long finger of a wave would flick, pull and roll the unsuspecting bather under the dark surface never to be seen again. Under the waves, dark and mysterious powers churned where no one, not even the bravest of the brave would dare dive on a night like this. They lurked and laid in waiting for someone or something to swallow whole and imprison in a watery cell.

The beach was no better. Like a giant hand it scooped up bushels of sharp edged sand and flung it, pelting anything that stood in its way. Pi's head was whipped and battered. Clumps of it became embedded in the corners of her eyes and under the thin layer of her exposed feathers. Driftwood tossed in the shallows of the Channel leapt and jumped onto the beach. The wind gathered all its strength and tried to pull Pi out of her sandy enclave. As she slept, the water crashed and pounded the surf; the lurkers laid in waiting, the winds blew and menaced all through the night, whistling tunes of danger.

The morning sky was a sailor's delight, bright clear and majestic. The Channel calmed and the powers under the currents vanished. The seascape stood up, shook itself like a big, blue and beige pastel colored blanket and gently settled itself into a painting.

Seagulls coasted high above the surf. They darted and dove. Saffron petals that had blown from the chalky cliffs the night before floated without direction in the gentle surf. Soon, fisherman with ruddy faces and coarse hands will row themselves in their small wooden boats out towards the morning catch, as a painter from a nearby village will set up easel and stand for hours of mixing and brushing colors in a vain attempt to capture a perfect Norman day.

The earthen sand beneath Pi's feet began to vibrate and hum. It started slowly and quietly and then grew with intensity and purpose as it rumbled and rattled until it pushed Pi up and out of her protective hole. The ground moved with great force and carried her in its wake. *What on earth is happening?* The beach set in motion, traveled towards the water's edge with Pi on its pebbled covered back encased in sand and stones. "Arrêtez!" Pi screamed but the beach had a mind of its own, it moved at a steady pace directly into the channel. Pi pushed with all her might trying to remove herself from the beach's grip, but the harder she tried the tighter the sand and stones clutched her. Her heart raced and again she cried out for help, "Aides-moi s'il vous plaît!" With no apparent escape from her perilous predicament the beach came to rest. Pi waited for something to happen, as the energy below her pulsated and beat like an idling engine. Then, like a volcano, it erupted and spit her into the air. She tumbled head over tail feathers and crashed directly back onto the mound that ejected her. She opened her eyes and two brown spheres sleepily stared out at her. She shrieked and gasped and stumbled backwards with her feet pointing towards the sky.

"Está loco," said the creature in the beach.

"What did you say?"

"I said, you're crazy. Why were you on my back? Why does everyone think that they can just come and sit on me whenever they feel like it? I don't go around sitting on others."

"Well, I'm sorry that…"

"What would it be like," he continued, "If everyone just sat wherever they felt like without ever looking at what or where he or she was sitting? Hmm, tell me?"

"I don't know for sure, but again…"

"Of course you don't know; that's because you're one of them."

"One of whom?"

"Have you not been listening to me? A sitter, that's 'whom'. One who sits on others or upon others' things or their belongings. It has become an epidemic."

Pi didn't know what to say or think. She had no idea what this creature was or what it was talking about.

"Now, if you would please pardon me I would like to go for my morning swim."

The great creature pushed himself from out of the sand, his tortoise-colored back coming into full view. He was gigantic. Weighing at least two hundred pounds he had massive feet and claws to match.

"May I ask, where and how can I get across the water to England?"

"Go to Cherbourg," the giant turtle said as he proceeded into the water.

"Pardonnez-moi?"

"Are you deaf too? I said Cherbourg. Go to Cherbourg. C-h-e-r-b-o-u-r-g! Now go and leave me be."

Chapter 15

"I CAN'T GO ON any longer, I just can't. I've tried père, I have really tried. Je suis très désolé." Pi dropped to her knees and tears filled her eyes. As she sat lost in thought and grief, a sound crept up from the distance. At first she thought it was one of the big machines that tried to sweep her from the Place de l'Étoile in Paris on the day she left home. She turned to look down the beach behind her and could barely make out the shape coming towards her. It moved at a rapid pace as it pounded out, *'Buh-dum, buh-dum, buh-dum, buh-dum.'* The sound became louder and louder and the shape larger and larger as it got closer and closer. *'Buh-dum, buh-dum, buh-dum, buh-dum.'* Sand from the beach swirled behind the image and the beach under her feet started to rattle and shake. Quickly, she burrowed herself in the sand, digging as fast as she could with her little claws. *'Buh-dum, buh-dum, buh-dum, buh-dum.'*

"Mon Dieu, I'm going to die here on the beach and I've come so far." She dug herself into the sand just as the sound came within a few meters from her hiding space. The sound quieted and the thousands of grains of sand surrounding her body settled into place. Only the crown of her head bore through the top.

A warm push of air parted the sparse feathers on her

head. Sounds of sniffing could be heard as another warm breath passed over her head puffing away sand and exposing her shoulders. Slowly she looked up into two round large and dark quivering holes. She gently pecked at the opening on her left and it pulled away revealing a very large face with big and friendly brown eyes.

"Bonjour. Je m'applle Big Fella."

"Bonjour," Pi said tentatively. She cocked her head so she could hear the ends of his words as they slowly slid and tumbled from his mouth. She thought to herself, *this is what mère must have meant when she told me that there are many different ways to speak the same language.* "Big Fella did you say?"

"Oui, Big Fella because I am the biggest cheval of all."

Pi had heard of horses but had never seen a real one before, only the ones on the carousel. Underneath layers of dust and sand Big Fella's hide was white except for a small brown patch that sat between his big expressive eyes. His frame was strong and impressive even though his ribs were poking through his skin.

"Enchanté. Je m'applle, Pi."

"Enchanté," replied Big Fella. "It is nice to meet you Pi. What brings you to Normandy?"

She was becoming pained explaining where and why she was going to seek Doctor Allbewell, but took the time to tell Big Fella the entire story.

After listening intently he swatted a sand fly with his tail and said, "Mademoiselle, you have journeyed such a long way on your own, you must be very tired."

"Big Fella, I have walked many miles and I must continue."

Gently kicking back the sand under his left front hoof, he asked, "Where is it that you need to go?"

"Cherbourg, I think. I was told that I can find a way across the Channel from there."

"Yes, that is true. I was once carted there myself. I can take you close to Cherbourg."

"That is very kind of you monsieur Big Fella, but you were obviously traveling in the opposite direction when you found me."

Big Fella batted his long soft eyelashes, pricked his ears forward, and bent down so that he was close to Pi. Close enough so that his warm breath enveloped and pushed her slightly back on her heels. "I want to help. I have four strong legs where you have just two. I can cover ten times the distance that you can in half the amount of time and be back here before you can say 'Vive la France!' Grab onto my mane and work your way onto my neck, and I will carry you into the sunset. Come, your chariot awaits!"

Pi followed Big Fella's instructions and perched herself atop his head sitting squarely between his long soft ears.

"Are you ready? He asked. "Hold on tight."

Before Pi could answer, Big Fella galloped down the beach at break-neck speed. Once she settled into the rhythm of Big Fella's strides, she relaxed her grip and started to enjoy the ride. They covered great distances at a very fast pace and arrived in Courceulles near the Arromanches. Big Fella slowed to a trot and then to a walk.

"Comment allez-vous?"

"Très parfait monsieur, merci. I am very grateful for the ride."

They continued their way up the beach taking in the beauty of the sea. Turquoise and pink light reflected on the clouds in the horizon as a crescent moon took shape in the northeastern sky. Pi knew that Big Fella could be a friend for life and felt comfortable with and trusted him.

"Monsieur Big Fella, may I ask you a personal question?"

"Oui mademoiselle. I have nothing to hide from you."

"Quel est votre famille?"

Big Fella stopped dead in his tracks. His left front and right back hoofs were suspended in mid stride. He stood perfectly still, as if painted into the landscape. Pi knew she struck a cord of pain that went deep into his hide.

"Big Fella, ça va? Are you alright?"

He didn't move a muscle; only the hair from his blonde mane tossed back and forth over his long neck as it shimmered in the wind. He broke his silence and stance with a neigh and began to walk slowly as he told Pi his family story.

"When she was young, my mother was a beautiful mare. She was brought to France from America with the hope to breed her with a Norman cheval. In his day, my father was a strong and fast stallion who roamed wild over Brittany before his freedom was stolen by poachers and his fate sealed after he met my mother in a old breeding farm near Trouville. From the moment they set eyes on each other they knew that they were soul mates and laid their heads across each other's necks.

"I was born soon after and my parents were so proud. They told everyone about their 'handsome and strong colt.' It was a bit embarrassing." Big Fella smiled with the telling of the memory but it faded quickly as he described in painstaking detail how early one morning four terrible men came and put a chain around his father's neck and pulled him out of the barn and tried to lock him in a metal truck.

"These men were so mean and ruthless and they didn't try to hide it. They acted like my father couldn't feel the rough treatment they inflected upon him. To them he was just another piece of hide they needed to move. But my father wasn't about to go into that metal truck without a fight. He kicked and neighed as hard as he could, but it was no use. The men punched, poked, and whipped him until he bled from his flanks.

"My mother cried and kicked on her stall door until it came crashing down in splinters and she screamed telling me to get out of the barn and gallop to the top of the mountain where she would meet me later but I didn't want to leave her and my father. She bolted out of the stall and stood high on her rear legs and repeatedly kicked and stomped the men that were trying to take my father away. The men held one of their free hands in front of their faces like scared little boys as they cowered under my mother. My father ripped the chain from the men's other hands and pulled away leaving their leather gloves ripped and torn. The three of us bolted from the barn and headed up to the top of the hill where we huddled under a rotting oak tree trying to catch our breath. We foamed with sweat and our hearts pounded from galloping so fast that I thought mine would pop out of my chest. We puffed and snorted and my father said that we should go deeper into the hills to where the forest was thick and there would be places to hide. We moved quickly up the hill over rocks and fallen trees until we came to the crest. It was a long way down the other side of the hill. Down and down we walked, down a long, steep slope that led to a shallow creek where we drank muddy water. We traveled like this for many days, eating whatever we could and resting under the cover of night, always looking over our backs for those men.

For months we lived like our ancestors, roaming the land in peace and freedom. Until one afternoon a man in a sky machine spotted us and chased us for miles until we ran into a deep bowl made of sharp and jagged cliffs. The sky machine was big and it trapped us and made so much powder from the dirt in the bowl that we could hardly see. Then men riding atop strong and well fed brothers and sisters charged at us with glaring and burning red eyes, determined faces and circles of ropes swinging over their heads. They threw their circles out and into the air and two of them fell around my mother's neck, and the men pulled her hard to the ground. My father stood on his hind legs and hollered and spat white foam trying to help her.

"Big Fella!" my mother cried out. "Run!" I just stood there angry and afraid looking at her suffering in the dirt with those ropes grinding and burning into her neck. My father commanded me, "Big Fella, va! Go! We will find you. Run!!"

And just as he said that a rope went around his neck and another around his hind legs binding him, and he too was pulled to the ground next to my mother. Then one of the men from the stable, the one who put the chain around my father's neck months before came and stood on my father's tail while he yelled and hollered into the sky like a sick coyote."

Big Fella stopped walking and scanned the Channel with his dark eyes. A long time passed before Pi softly asked, "What did you do?"

"Nothing, I was helpless. There were so many men and just one me. Both my mother and father screamed to me to run. They promised we would be together again. They promised over and over...

"Mademoiselle, I don't know if my parents are alive. I don't know what happened to them. I've asked everyone, but I have no answers to my questions."

Sand flies buzzed and small waves from the Channel crashed to the shore as they walked towards Cherbourg. Neither of them spoke for many miles. Seagulls cried and yelped as they fought over small pieces of decaying shellfish. All the while Pi and Big Fella walked in silence.

As they neared Cherbourg Pi spoke first, "Monsieur Big Fella, I am truly sorry for you and your family, and I thank you for sharing your story with me."

She wanted to say more because she felt she should, that if she did she'd make everything right for him, heal his sadness, cure his pain. Pi knew what so many days and nights away from his mother and father had done to his soul.

"You want to ask me something don't you? I can tell. Go ahead, ask."

"It's nothing really."

Big Fella turned his head around to look at Pi on his long neck. The way he gazed at her reminded her of the way her father had always lovingly looked at her.

"You and I have come from a similar place. I've told you more than I have ever told anyone else. So, what is it?"

"Well…what I want to ask you is this. How do you keep going on day after day? You've been without your mother and father for so long now. Do you ever become really afraid?"

Big Fella lowered his head and Pi slid to the sandy beach. He put his face close to hers like he had when they first met. "Of course I get afraid sometimes, we all do. Anybody who says different is lying. It takes a whole mountainside of courage to show the world your entire self and not just the parts that you want them to see. So being afraid and not trying to hide it means in some kind of strange way that you're not afraid at all."

"Are you angry at them for not coming back?"

"I was angry for a very long time, so much so that I couldn't eat or sleep or do much of anything else except to kick and scream at anything and everything. But not anymore. Time has its way with you one way or another and it just didn't make sense to stay angry any longer. Besides, I was getting too hungry and too tired from not eating and sleeping."

Pi managed a slight smile and turned to face the setting sun as it fell behind the water's edge. Big Fella took a step closer toward her, being careful not to stomp her. There the two of them, big and small, stood watching the sun fade as it cast their shadows behind them and up the beach. Big Fella turned to Pi with a knowing look on his handsome face. "Did you know Pi that horses have a sixth sense? Some say maybe even a seventh sense."

"No, I did not know that."

"Well, it's true mademoiselle and I have a sense about you."

"You do? And what does it tell you?"

He leaned his head down and looked directly into Pi's pale orange colored eyes. "I think that maybe you're a bit angry yourself."

She thought that was a strange thing to say. She was sad

yes, lonely even, but angry? No. "Why would I be angry? I think that maybe your sixth sense is wrong today. I'm not angry. What would I have to be angry about?"

"Maybe you're angry about having to come all this way by yourself. Or maybe you're angry too about your père being sick and your having to be so far from home."

She felt punched in the stomach. Somewhere, deep down and hidden away, a piece of that anger touched her soul. "No, I'm not angry."

"Maybe I'm mistaken. I had a feeling and it usually isn't wrong." He turned and started to walk away giving her a piece of the beach to herself.

"Big Fella, wait."

"Oui, mademoiselle?"

"It's true. I don't want it to be true, but I am angry." She turned towards the Channel to hide the tears forming in her eyes. Big Fella sauntered next to her, his tail waving side to side. His right hindquarters twitched shaking off a few night mosquitoes.

"Thank you, Pi. Thank you for reminding me."

"Of what?"

"The tremendous amount of courage it sometimes takes to be yourself."

"I don't know if it's courage or fear that's kept me going."

"Courage wouldn't exist without fear."

She contemplated his words and said, "Yes, I guess that's true. I've never thought about fear going before courage."

"There's something else."

"Yes?"

"When you return to Paris start doing all the things that you've been afraid to do."

She was slightly offended and turned her face half towards the sea. "And what is it that you think that I have been afraid to do?"

"Only you can answer that."

She looked down at her feet and back to Big Fella. "Très bien. I will and hopefully I will be able to tell you about my new experiences one day."

The setting sun cast long shadows that followed Pi and Big Fella as they walked west. Their flat companions drifted and caressed the folds in the cool beige sands. Pi knew that her time with her unlikely friend was coming to an end. When they reached Le Becquet several miles from Cherbourg, Big Fella turned to Pi and said, "Well my friend, this is just about the end of the line. I'll take you to the water's edge at Cherbourg. It's a very long trip to the other side. How will you get there?"

"I don't know Big Fella, but I do know that you are one of the kindest animals I have ever met."

"Merci Pi, moi aussi. I have enjoyed your company and friendship more than you can imagine."

After their shadows completely vanished, the first stars in the night sky flickered. Big Fella sat down in the cooled sand, and Pi came round to face him.

"Monsieur, je suis heureuse de vous compter parmi mes amis et honorée que vous ayez partagé vos secrets avec moi. Permettez-moi de vous presenter tous mes voeux de Bonheur."

"Mademoiselle, I too am thankful for your friendship. I wish that you travel in peace, happiness and safety."

Big Fella couldn't allow for any more words to pass between them. He rose to his feet and trotted quickly down the beach until the last of his tail hairs brushed through the darkness and out of sight.

Chapter 16

DAYBREAK CAME WITH PI sitting and staring out at the sea, the same way she had the night before. Ten hours she sat and searched for an answer. The cold winds slowed, brought calmer weather but no solutions. It was too vast and she too small.

"Have I come all this way for nothing? Je ne comprends pas. How will I ever cross these waters? Oh Great One, what am I going do to? Oh, Bird…great, great bird…bird…bird… bird."

Pi appeared to be asleep while awake, repeating her mantra over and over with eyes fixed on the horizon, looking for something through the miles of sea and haze. She hadn't noticed that the sand beneath her feet began to dissolve into the Channel's encompassing embrace. The water rose under her wings, lifted her feet and carried her away from the shore and further out to sea.

The news that his estranged twin brother Pierre had died trickled down to Étienne via the Aqua-line. Pierre cut off the relationship on their fifteenth birthday; something trivial, as most siblings' arguments tend to be. Years later Pierre confessed that he couldn't even remember what he and Étienne had disagreed about, but by then the mixture of pride and time built up an impenetrable wall and neither brother was willing to remove the first brick.

Today would have been their collective twentieth birthday. Étienne's thoughts turned to his brother and the brief good times they had shared before parting ways. They had spent their days frolicking in oxygen-rich water, leaping, twirling and spinning through rivers, tributaries and streams. Friendly kings of the waterways, they befriended everyone. "Look, here come the brothers!" They would shout. "Hooray for Pierre and Étienne!" Now, all of Étienne's family were gone and he was left with a bellyful of sadness and remorse. He swam through the chilled waters of the Channel in a daze. Easy prey floated by his snout without his noticing. "What have I done? Why was I so stubborn? Why did I refuse to forgive?" He stopped in the middle of the Channel and slowly sank as he gulped water. And then he remembered something that Pierre had once told him when they were very young. "Étienne, you are my only brother and when the day comes that we see each other for the last time, remember that we will always be connected. Fin to fin, scale to scale, brothers until the end." Étienne quickly spit and flushed the water from his mouth and gills and rocketed towards the surface. As he broke through, his nose bumped against a lump of wet feathers. "Get off my face!" Etienne screamed. Pi was brought out from her sleep feeling a wet and rubbery object thrust into her tail feathers. Her feet reached out for solid ground until she realized that she was floating on the Channel.

"Will you please take your buttocks from off my face?!" Etienne's snout was caught in Pi's tail feathers. The more she twisted and turned the more entangled they became.

"Stop! Stop for just a minute," Étienne pleaded.

"Where are you?"

"Hmm, do you not feel a wet nose up your self?"

"I feel something uncomfortable in that area, yes. What are you doing with your nose there? What are you? Who are you?"

"Let's dispense with the salutations until we can actually see one another. That would be wise, don't you think?"

"Oui, I agree. Any ideas?"

"I was once caught in a fishing net with thousands of others and the more I struggled the more entangled I became."

"How did you manage to free yourself?"

"I don't know. Fighting so hard against the net I stopped breathing and the next thing I knew I was trolling the shoreline in a daze."

"That's it."

"That's what?"

"Pardonez-moi. What is your name?"

"Étienne. And yours?"

"Pi."

"Enchanté."

"Enchanté, monsieur Étienne."

"Oui?"

"Non, I was not asking a question. I was just saying your name."

"As I told you, my name is Étienne."

"Yes, I know, Étienne."

"Oui?"

"Non."

"Non?"

"Non. Non! I mean oui! Yes, your name is Étienne. We have established that and I am Pi."

"Oui, Pi?"

"Arret!" Her frustration boiled over. "Arrêtez! Arrêtez! Arrêtez! Arrêtez! Arrêtez! Arrêtez!" As she wailed she unknowingly beat her wings so hard that they lifted her from off the surface of the Channel. Étienne broke free from his unexpected bondage.

"Mademoiselle. We are free of each other." But Pi continued to scream, "Arrêtez! Arrêtez t! Arrêtez!"

"Mademoiselle! Mademoiselle. "Arrêtez yourself! Arrêtez!"

Étienne's call was finally heard, and Pi sank back into the Channel. She gulped buckets of water before she righted herself and for the first time saw Étienne's face.

"Pierre? Mon Dieu! Pierre, comment saviez-vous…? I saw you…on the coast…I saw you…" She broke down into a thousand tears that raised the water's level higher and higher. Pierre's face turned a whitish-gray as his gills paused pumping oxygen.

"Mademoiselle, I am not Pierre. Mademoiselle, do you hear me? Écouter! I am not Pierre!"

"How could it not be? You are Pierre."

"Non, non, I am not. Pierre was my brother. He…how do you know Pierre? He was killed at…"

Pi's face flushed with embarrassment. "Je suis désolé. I am so sorry Monsieur. You look…"

"Exactly alike?"

"Yes. Exactly."

"How did you know my brother?"

Pi recounted their journey together and of Pierre's bravery and courage. She told Étienne of his brother's kind and generous heart and how he gave his life for hers. And when she finished she saw that Étienne lay motionless with only his eyes peeking out from the surface. "I am so very sorry Monsieur. So very sorry."

Pierre blinked twice and then swished his tail left to right and said, "C'est la vie. I heard of my brother's death earlier…so many years…"

"Your brother was…well…"

"Yes, I know that now."

Pierre cleared his throat and asked, "What brings you my flying friend to the middle of the Sea?"

"The last I remember I was on the beach over there and I am on my way there." She pointed towards France.

"You are headed to France?"

"Non, I am going to England."

"You are a bit confused. England is that way." He turned his snout towards the beaches of Ventnor. "La, that is the closest point."

"Ah, merci."

"You will be on your way now, I suppose?"

"Yes."

"Très bien. It was nice to meet you."

"It was a pleasure to meet the brother of one of the kindest fishes I have ever had the pleasure of meeting."

Pierre gave Pi some room to take flight. "If you are ever in need of anything, please, do not hesitate to ask."

"Merci. That is very kind of you Monsieur Pierre."

They waited for each other: Pierre for Pi to take flight and Pi for Pierre to disappear into the distance.

"Mademoiselle?"

"Oui?"

"Do you need help now?"

She blushed. "You are as kind as your brother. Yes, I do need assistance. It would be most appreciated if…"

"Say no more. To the shores of England we shall go!"

Like his brother, Étienne carried Pi, this time across the Channel. As they approached St. Catherine's Point a flash storm erupted and threw slashes of rain down on the Channel. Étienne instinctively dove below the surface and left Pi to face the thunderous storm alone. When the weather lifted and the fog parted, the shoreline once again came into view. Several miles separated Pi and the closest land mass. She bobbed hopelessly for hours until she came to rest on a sheet of plywood that was moored to a rotted and toppled pier at the Isle of Wight.

Amongst the moss-covered timbers a lone Skylark with matted brown plumage mumbled a haunting refrain:

"You with the soft feathers kneeling by the drain
alone and shivering in the rain.
Your call to mother went unanswered and it was me
who spoke with words of sorrow and pain.
If only I would have yielded, bent to your simple plea
but I was drunk on bravado and riotous glee.
If only I had stayed instead of flying off to that parade.
All those times you tried to persuade - almost a crusade
should have caused me my love to have stayed."

The Skylark stopped his verse and sighed then began again. He repeated this routine until the wind shifted and he heard Pi scratching her head.

"You there lass. What are you doing there lurking?"

"I was not lurking Monsieur, I didn't want to disturb you."

"Monsieur? So you're French are you?"

"Oui."

"Well, I won't hold that against you."

"Yes, I am French and quite proud." She eyed him with caution as he rose to his feet. "Would you please tell me sir, do you know a bird of the name, Allbewell?"

The Skylark dropped to his knees. He looked as if someone had punched him in the stomach. "Allbewell…Allbewell."

"Do you know him?"

"Allbewell, Allbewell, I know him well. He is the reason that I am…" He caught himself before sharing too much. "Don't ask. I know what you want to ask and I am tired of telling the same story over and over."

"I know exactly how you feel Monsieur."

"You do?"

"Yes, I do."

"Why did you come here lass?" She didn't answer. Ah, I see, touché. No need to share your story with me."

"Monsieur, could you please tell me where I can find Dr. Allbewell?"

"Doctor? I didn't know that he was a doctor." He mumbled to himself, "A doctor of what I wonder."

"Pardon?"

"Nothing little lass, nothing." He stood and lifted his pointed beak. "The last I heard of *Doctor* Allbewell was that he was living in seclusion on the Isle of Wight. Godshill maybe. And if you ask me that's exactly where he should stay."

"I don't know what happened between you and Doctor Allbewell, but I appreciate your help. Merci, merci beaucoup."

The Skylark began to sing a heavy and mournful song with all the weight of a stone that had been flung from a river's shoreline, skimmed the surface and then plummeted to the sandy riverbed.

"Monsieur, I have never heard anything so sad in all my life. I am very sorry for whatever happened to have caused you so much pain and sorrow."

His dark mood suddenly lifted. "Aye lass…thank you and may the winds always be at your back."

"Merci. Would you mind very much telling me which direction to the Isle of Whight?"

"Go northwest flying over the Highland Road until the tall grasses grow shorter and then you'll find a stone guide. Go in the direction of the guide's left wing and then head north at 50.5932°N 1.3041°W, or is that fifty-five degrees South? Well, never-the-knell it shall befell you when you know it least."

"Excuse me?"

"For what?

"I meant what did you mean by, "Never-the-knell…?"

He quickly interrupted her and snorted through is beak, ""Never-the-knell" lass is an ole' English countryside saying which in plain bird speak means, the bell may ring but you can't count on knowing who rang it."

"Hmm, I'll ponder that for awhile."

"You do that lass, you do that. Now, if that's all I can do you for I'd like to drift back into the depression of the thought from whence you took me from."

"But you appeared to be feeling better why the....?"

"Aye, no more. My moods change quicker than the Channel's winds. Leave now."

He dropped back into his remorseful refrain repeating it softly under his breath. His words were masked with ripped and torn gauze, which long ago lost their restorative capacities. "If only I would have...bent to your simple plea but I was drunk on bravo...riotous glee. If only I had stayed instead of flying off..."

Circles round and circles square, around again and square no more, walk round to you come to the bend where once again you will begin again.

Disheveled, hungry, and very tired, Pi walked on through Ventor, Bierley, Nettlecombe, Roud, and a misstep that led to Challe Green and back to Roud again. She landed upon Godshill at All Saints' Church where there, at the top of the church's Saxon cornice, stood a black crow on one leg delivering one last set of directions.

"Hear there and hear everywhere, to the hallowed tree and cross roads yonder," he crowed.

"Cross roads?"

"There."

Pi looked down the gravel road then back to the crow but he was gone from his perch. She followed the road until it forked and in the middle of the branches of Church Hallow and Church Hill, a sturdy two hundred year old maple stood behind a grass-thatched house in the shadow of the All Saints Church. A sheer curtain of tiny green diamonds gleamed and shimmered in the afternoon sun, enveloping house and tree alike. Unlike the spitefully cold Channel winds the air here was inviting.

Twenty feet up the tree, ensconced in the center of its trunk was a well-worn and comfortable nesting hallow. Scratches from years of comings and goings of the nest's inhabitants were etched deep around the small entrance.

Pi stood and stretched her neck searching the tree for signs of the good Doctor. A soft wind blew and the tree's leaves shuttered. A flutter of bee's wings buzzed her ears and an alley cat picked up her presence through the tips of his long and sensitive whiskers. He tiptoed through hedgerows aiming for a better view of what might become his afternoon tea.

All the time, all the miles walked and now, here, standing in blades of countryside grass, Pi's beak was, as, the locals would say, "beak smacked."

There were echoes. Echoes past, echoes present. Stinking hellebore and the creamy white faces of climbing corydalis echoed their wind-swept brethren's collective journeys from seeds to sprouts, sprouts to bloom. With defiant and stubborn stems, they defied anyone to crush and break them.

Pi took a deep breath and a step closer to the tree and called out, "Doctor Allbewell?" A wayward stonechat lifted his head from padding the family's nest in a neighboring tree, looked down at the stranger and then went back to work. She called for Doctor Allbewell again but there was no response.

She kicked the grass at her feet and a grasshopper leapt out. "Je suis vraiment désolé," Pi apologized.

"Think nothing of it. I was just about to jump over to the cousin's house. On my way now." He flicked his thin legs and vanished.

Something stirred from within the tree. First a hum then a quick, *click-tap, click-tap* was heard.

Pi looked up to the opening in the tree. "Hello?

Click-tap, click-tap.

"Hello? Is there anyone up there?"

The cat near the hedgerows mistakenly stepped on a twig and cracked it. Pi turned around to face the now hissing cat. She pointed her beak and lifted her wings. The cat screeched and ran back through the thickets.

"That'll teach him." Proud of herself, she turned back to the tree and firmly called, "Doctor Allbewell, if you are up there would you please make yourself known? I am here on a matter of life and death."

From the nest in the tree an even-pitched voice laced with age and confidence said, "Archibald, I've told you once, I've told you thrice, not to bother the neighbors." A smoky gray beak poked through the hole in the tree and pointed down to the ground as if it had eyes of its own. "Archibald, what sort of trouble have you gotten yourself into today? Archibald? We agreed that when you came here that I was not going to replace your father but that you would at least listen to my guidance. You know how much it irritates me when you ignore me," he mumbled to himself. "I do know Archibald that you behave like this to purposely irritate me… Archibald?" A face with deep-set almond colored eyes ringed with the onset of glaucoma appeared through the nest's round entrance. Black and white checkered shoulders barely squeezed through the opening. "Well, who do we have here?" He said looking down at Pi.

She looked at him and was speechless. After all the miles traveled, here in the middle of this tall tree in the middle of this little island paradise, all she could manage was a weak, "Bonjour."

"Well, bonjour to you as well, I'm certain of it. Well, you are certainly not Archibald. Did he frighten you miss? I have instructed that poor lad many times not to frighten anyone, even at play. He doesn't realize how he can scare the bejesus out of us. Sometimes he can be so buffle-headed."

"No, I think that I frightened him."

He let out a hardy laugh and said, "Good for you. Very good for you!"

"Merci Monsieur, merci." She smiled with a slight nod of her head.

"Where are my manners? I am going to come down and introduce myself properly." He tried to push his body through the hole but his wings were pressed too tight against the sides. "Oh, it seems I've been eating a bit too much lately." He wiggled and shimmied and managed to extricate half of his rotund body from the tree. He chuckled at his own predicament, "Oh, ha, ha, ha tee-hee. Would you look at me? You would think that after all the lecturing I've given all my patients over the years that…" He inhaled a deep breath and his remaining proportions popped through the opening. "Ah, that's better. Here I come." He took one step off the edge and gracefully glided down to Pi.

Getting on in years, Doctor Allbewell's carriage was a bit shorter, his belly a bit tubbier and his chest feathers more gray. His face was kind and gentle, as one would have imagined after having devoted his entire life to the care of others. He carried the usual markings of a checkered except for the color of his legs, which were different; like mismatched pants. One, gray the other white. Somewhat more unusual were the feathers that curled down his legs onto the top of his feet, helping him to look like he wore spats. The rest of him was a checkered through and through. Some said that he's a bit absent-minded but all agreed that he's sharp as an eagle's talon. How both can be accurate is anyone's guess but the truth is, absent-minded or not, the good doctor is smart and brilliant and one might take him to be a bit distracted at times but if they knew all that he had to remember: special remedies, potions and salves; they too, would appear to be absent-minded.

Similar to Pi, he was his parent's only child and in having been, he received all of their attention. Their focus helped to nurture a caring, loving and dedicated son, friend and comrade. He was a flight scout before offering his services to help keep the world intact during the War. He never managed to marry, not because he wouldn't have made a good spouse, quite the contrary, he would have been the perfect husband. But his oath to help and heal always took precedence over his own needs and he never had nor took the time to lay the foundation required for an intimate relationship. He said it best, "My pestle and mortar could cure what ailed others but no matter how powerful and effective, a marriage they could not create." He did though, manage to fill a passionate yearning years ago during an intense affair with a beautiful brown-faced skylark, who after five months of splendor, tearfully revealed that she had promised herself to another. The brokenhearted doctor sought refuge in the nook of the old maple tree and the skylark's husband sought solace in taking his revenge.

"Ah, that's better. Now, whom do we have here? Let's get a good look at you." He looked Pi up and down with the utmost care and attention from tail to crown pausing to notice the differences in her wing's symmetry and then once again at the bright blue streak running through her breast feathers. He gasped, "Oh Lord! I haven't seen that pattern of feathers in quite some time." A well-worn image of long lost friends appeared before him and he asked, "Are you in anyway related to…?"

"Je m'appelle Pi Phillecroix."

The doctor stumbled backwards and shook his tail and head feathers. After gathering himself he bowed which caused his knees to creak. "I am honored mademoiselle, honored."

"The honor is all mine doctor."

"Are you the daughter of mes amis Paul and Piette Phillecroix?"

"I am. Are you Doctor Allbewell?"

"Yes, I am Doctor Allbewell!"

His head was swimming with questions and a bit of guilt for not having kept in touch with his old friends for all these years. "Mademoiselle how are your dear parents? Where are they? Are they still in Paris? What brings you here to our little island?"

"Doctor Allbewell, I am here because of my father."

"Oh no, don't tell me. Has he…"

"Non. Well, I do not know for certain, as I have been traveling for so long. Doctor Allbewell, my père is very sick. Mère tried a remedy from the forest but it had no effect."

"Ah, your mother was always very industrious and a great medical assistant when called upon by the Resistance."

"Mère said that you are the only one that could save père if, at…" She dropped her head and began to cry.

"Oh, there, there lass. Let it all out." Doctor Allbewell spread his wings wide and enveloped her like a warm feathered blanket and she melted into his wings. "There, there…Ah, yes, that's it lass. You let it all go Doctor Allbewell is here and all will be well."

Pi inhaled a deep breath and with it came the wondrous feeling of belonging; just a small but essential part of a large symphony. She chuckled thinking what he just said, "Doctor Allbewell is here and all will be well. That is very funny."

"That's true, it is funny and I am glad to see that you have not lost your sense of humor."

"I'm sorry Doctor Allbewell, I usually do not lose my

composure so easily."

"There is no need to apologize mademoiselle. I can only begin to imagine how you're feeling. Once, when I was a young man…well, that doesn't matter a nit. Let's go up to the nest for a much needed rest."

Doctor Allbewll took a step towards the old maple tree. When he noticed that Pi was not following he said, "Ah come on lass. It's all right. It's not much but it's a home. There's nothing to be frightened about."

"I can't."

"Oh your parents did instill such wonderful and virtuous values in you, didn't they?" He laughed and continued, "I'm just an old bird now, you can certainly trust me."

"It's not that Doctor Allbewell. Of course I trust you. It's just that I can't get up to the nest.

"What do you mean that you can't get up to the nest? I assure you that it's safe and comfortable. Come on now, I want to hear more about your père."

"Yes, I am certain that it is; however, I cannot fly to the nest. I have never been able to fly Dr. Allbewell."

His faced filled with astonishment. He had witnessed countless examples of the Phillecroix' aerial expertise and was privy to their desire and hope to bear offspring that would carry on the family name and flying excellence. "I…I..I am," He stuttered and then regained his composure. "Good Lord. Where are my senses?!" He looked skyward and hollered, "Senses, come back to me senses. I really need you now." He looked back to Pi and saw a slight smile take shape on her now pale face. "Looking at me you'd think I just saw the Great Golden Bird swoop down from the heavens!"

"That is the second time that…" Pi thought that he might be teasing her and she thought back to the beaches of Normandy.

"Second time for what lass?"

"It's nothing."

"Mademoiselle, there is no need to explain. We shall stay right here under the leafy and protective arms of our rooted friend."

Dr. Allbewell spit a seed between his weathered beak and said, "It's been quite some time since I've flown myself."

Pi waited for him to give more details, that what he really meant was that he hadn't flown long distances in quite some time. But her pause turned into an uncomfortable gap where the good doctor being good and understanding said, "I know what you're thinking mademoiselle."

"Je suis désolé Doctor Allbewell. I wasn't judging, I was thinking only…"

"It's okay lass, tis' really okay. My wings still work, it's my heart that's lost some of its fire." He looked away and continued, "Seems the older I get the less brave I become. Should be the opposite don't you think?"

Pi smiled. She knew that he wasn't expecting an answer.

"Time was I got so cankered with myself for not having the stuff I had when I was a young bird. Oh, you should have seen me back then flying here and there and all over the world." He looked skyward. "I was considered quite the flyer then, I was. Sharp, fierce and determined they said I was and I guess a bit of that was true, especially if someone needed my help. I took my oath to help and heal very seriously; still do as a matter of fact. Your parents could attest to that much."

"They have Doctor Allbewell. They have told me so much about you and how wonderfully courageous you were during the War. I know that you saved my père's life at the risk of losing your own. And I know that you risked your life for many others as well." She faced him so that he couldn't avoid her eyes. "Dr. Allbewell, courage is not something that you lose like a breadcrumb that you tucked away in your feathers. It may be hidden but it is still there, inside you."

"Ah, you sounded just like your mother there, you did.

Always the one to be encouraging others, always positive, the one who finds the sunshine in a hail storm."

"I guess that I do sound just like her. She has said the same thing to me many times when I was younger. She told me that I always know…" Doctor Allbewell finished the sentence for her, "Know the way." She said the same to me many times as well when I didn't think that I'd be able to find my way through the War's smoke and fire. "You know the way, you know the way," she'd say."

"Oui, oui, oui," Pi said laughing. "She's been right so far, I finally found you."

"How long have you been traveling?"

"I'm not quite sure Doctor Allbewell, it seems like a very long time since I left our nest atop l'Arc de Triomphe. I stopped counting the sun's settings and the moon's risings somewhere outside of Paris."

"It doesn't matter now. You're here and I need to know your father's symptoms in detail so that I can send you back with the proper remedy."

Pi's face fell with disappointment. "Doctor Alllbewell, mon père cannot wait for me to walk all the way back to des Champs Élyséses; it maybe too late already. Please Doctor Allbewell, please fly to him right now. Please?" Doctor Allbewell looked perplexed and anxious, caught between two clouds. "You won't go will you? You're not going to go, are you?"

"Aye, lass, tis' not that I don't want to go…it's just that I haven't…I haven't left the nest in a very long time. These ole' wings of mine I'm afraid to say, well, I'm afraid that I…well, I think that you understand?"

"Non. Non, I do not understand. You are a doctor and a member of your flock is ill. Your friend, Paul Phillecroix is sick and needs your help and so you must fly to him."

He was impressed with her determination and it appeared very familiar. "I see you've got some of your mother's resolve too."

She nodded and then asked, "What happened to you Doctor Allbewell? You've lost something haven't you?"

He rolled his tongue to the roof his mouth and held it there for a few seconds buying himself some time before he answered. When he relaxed it, it created a slight smacking sound. "Ah lass, that smarts a bit."

"Doctor Allbewell, I didn't mean to…"

He quickly interrupted her, "No, no, 'tis okay. You've hit the mark, spot on. I may be scorched a wee bit but you found something that's true." He tucked his wings tightly to his body and sighed and then leveled his head. "Aye, I've lost something. I've lost my self-belief. I've been sitting in this tree for so long and haven't ventured further than the hedgerows. Seems that everything I've needed has been under and around this wonderful old tree. The longer I stay, the less I want to leave." He lowered his head and as he did, a swift wind blew from the south and lifted the tips of his tail feathers. He muttered to himself, "One's work is never finished."

"Pardon?"

"I have become complacent my dear friend and as they say, "Complacency is the friend of…" He looked to his right then to his left. "Complacency is the friend of the…of the…"

"Friend of the devil?" Pi offered.

"No, that's not it."

"Friend of the conceited?"

"Hmm, no. Not that either."

"Arrogant?"

"No, not arrogant."

"Pardonnez-moi, Doctor Allbewell but is this of absolute importance?"

"Ah! I remember! 'Complacency is friends with vanity.'" Proud of himself, he puffed out his chest and snorted through his nostrils, "My body may be knackered but my mind however is as quick as ever."

"Doctor Allbewell, can you reach Paris by sunset?"

Heat surged through his feet and up through his legs with the thought of leaving the nest and the old maple tree. "I'm not sure that I can. I'm just not sure."

"Yes you can," She looked at him squarely in his eyes and commanded, "You can and you must."

He looked at Pi through his watery eyes and knew that he had to go; he had to face the fears that had been building inside of him for so many years. Surely he could make one more flight. Maybe his last but he had to make this one. His memory wouldn't let him escape Paul Phillecroix darting through a hail of bullets to save his life as he was trying to save another's. All of his training, the thousands of miles flown, would help get him across the big, wide sea. He had to tell himself this.

"Doctor Allbewell?"

"Yes, dear?"

"My parents were broken when they learned I couldn't fly. They had waited so long."

"I'm sure they were and are still very proud of you, yes?"

"Oui, they are. When they took me to the bottom of l'Arc so that they could pass on their skills to me, ones that I would never possess, even then, they loved me." She shifted her weight to her right leg. "You have to fly. You can not sacrifice that gift just because you're afraid." She was surprised by her tone. She flapped her wings and as they beat she wobbled and commanded Doctor Allbewell, "Allez! Do it. Flap." He reluctantly began to lift his wings unevenly and then slowly fluttered them and the years of neglect caused him to say, "Oh, I am a wee bit sore mademoiselle."

"Keep flapping," Pi tapped out orders like a drill sergeant, "Flap, un, deux, trois, flap. Allez, une, duex, trios, flap. That's it Doctor. Oui, flap, un, deux, trois, flap."

The repeated motion of lifting his wings then lowering

them to his back caused his heart to pound and his temperature to rise. The pleasures of flying came back to him and he said with glee, "Aye, this is good my dear friend. This is very good indeed. I've missed the sound of my feathers beating together and the air under my wings. Thank you Pi, thank you!"

"Why don't you take a circle flight, Doctor Allbewell?"

"That's a fine idea, a fine idea."

He stepped forward, pushed off and became airborne. He flew over and around All Saints' Church and Church Hallow and Church Hill and Trickling Creek and Bob's Head Farm and Emma's Curve. All the joy, all the wonderful sensations of flight came back. All. And so too, did the ease that comes with instinct; the effortlessness, the happiness. Pi saw it from the ground. She recognized it in the way he soared; relaxed, in the same way her parents were when they took their carefree after dinner flights, hovering close to the top of the l'Arc de Triomphe inches from her adolescent head.

Doctor Allbewell floated on a warm thermal and called out with strain and remorse, "Oh Maureen, you and I were so serene. Why ever did you leave? Why did you go when you did? Could I have done anything that would have prevented you from going back to him? Could I have tried harder, wooed you more, cooed you with a sweeter song?" He couldn't have done anything differently. She would have gone back to her skylark no matter what he tried. He knew that she hadn't intended to hurt him; her only fault was that she let her passions get in the way of her honesty. "Maureen, if only you would have told me the truth earlier, my heart may not have shattered to so many pieces."

The sun glared into his eyes bringing him back to the present. "Aye, never-the-knell. It matters no more. Too many years lay between then and now." He adjusted his wings, leaned to the left and glided down to Pi.

"That lass, was wonderful! I'd forgotten how wonderful it

was."

She looked at him, her face shaped a question. He tamped down one of his tail feathers with his beak and then met her eyes. "Ah, that was grand lass, grand." Pi said nothing, she waited for Doctor Allbewell to give her his decision. "Oh, I see. Yes, yes, yes, you want to know if I'll go." He waddled a few steps closer to the Maple tree and pecked at a lone seed at its roots. "Hmm…hmm…hmm." He spun on one heel to Pi and said, "Oui, of course I'll go. I will not, cannot leave your father in distress. It is my duty. I shall leave at once!"

All of Pi's walking; all of the cold and lonely nights; the days without eating, were now, at least in part, worth their weight in gold.

"Merci Doctor Allbewell, merci beaucoup."

"Ah, lass. There's no need for tears. You've come too far for tears now. Wait until you see me fly towards the Channel and then you'll have something to cry about. An old bird with old muscles and old feathers flying lopsided across the great waters, that, will give you something to cry about!"

"Thank you Doctor Allbewell. Please, please go now. Hopefully I will see you in Paris before you leave."

"I will go at it with vlux." He pronounced the word with a deep and heavy emphasis on the u and x. "With thunder and the speed of lightening. No, I shall not dither any longer. I am off to help your father. See you there. Travel safe, travel with no…"

"Vlux?"

"Aye no time to explain. Just a little word from our little island." He was about to take flight when he remembered something, "Archibald! I almost forgot about Archibald. Please, mademoiselle, should you see that wayward cat tell him that I shant be too long. Tell him to stay clear of the robin's nest." He leaned his head and said in a low voice, "They did a real doozey on his nose last time he tried to steal their eggs, they did."

"Doctor Allbewell, please."

"Yes, of course. I do dither on. I shall engage the winds and may they carry me swiftly to your père and mère and all shall be well." He was about to push off then asked, "Wait! But what about you? How will you get home? I can't leave you here."

"I have come all this way on my own and I will return on my own."

"No, no, this won't do. It won't do at all."

"Doctor Allbewell, please leave now. I will do my best to get there as quickly as I can. It is more important that you help my father."

"Okay love, okay. There's no persuading you, is there?"

"Non."

"Well then, off I go." He pushed off and took a southeast turn and shouted over his shoulder, "Au revoir mon amie."

Pi raised her left wing and said, "Bon voyage, Doctor." She watched as he flew further away; his shape grew smaller and smaller until it became a pinpoint on the horizon and then it too, was gone.

Chapter 17

To BE FULFILLED AND empty at the same time is quite an unusual state. Pi didn't understand it. On one wing, she had completed what she had set out to do; on the other, she had no idea if her efforts would help her father and if she'd ever see him or her mother again. It's like tasting the sweet nectar of a summer's peach that recently dropped from its branch – you peck at it, suck its juice until it's dry. Then you look around to find that there are no more peaches. All the peach trees are bare and your belly is full but what will you eat tomorrow?

Pi stumbled in a moment of lost direction, suspended on a blank page. Fourteen monarch butterflies waltzed passed her, their wings gently fanned her head. "Hello there miss." "Top of the day." "Fine day for flying, don't you agree?" She watched and listened as they flew off over the hedgerows and marveled over how free they appeared.

"It's time to go home." She was resolved, even though her face showed the well-worn path she had traveled. She looked back at Church Hallow and Church Hill Roads and sighed. After contemplating her route she took the first step back to Paris and the l'Arc de Triomphe. Thoughts of seeing her family again boosted her spirits and she hastened her pace until she reached All Saints' Church where the black crow on one leg was back at the top of the cornice, this time stammering about the weather. "If you could be got by the rain and the storm and you wanted to be got which would you be got by?"

"Does it really matter? If I can't get home what difference does it make about the weather?"

"There will be someone there who will be there to ride you home."

"What are you saying? Who will ride me home?"

"There." He pointed with his beak to the sky.

"Where? I don't see anyone. Who is coming?" She looked back to the crow but he was gone from his perch. The sun began to set. She decided not to leave the little island at night. She'd be fresh, rested, determined in the morning, and perhaps, a bit more courageous as well.

Starlings, brown finches, yellowhammers, and one lone barn owl, woke Pi singing their favorite melodies. A flock of barheaded geese looking like bars of chocolate and vanilla-striped ice cream flew overhead, honking their passing. A sign of good or bad to come was seen in a rare, wandering and lost masked booby.

"No time to talk, no time at all," the masked booby spat out as she waddled off into the distance.

Pi wasted no time and rose quickly to her feet and headed off towards the Channel. Of all the places she thought she would have landed in, this was not one of them. She retraced the path that she came from, down past Saint Catherine's Point, past the heart torn poet where he rhapsodized self-loathing, until she stood face-to-face with friend and formidable opponent, the great waters of the Channel. It saw her coming long before she saw it. It lay like a sleeping giant. It could make or take your life with little effort. It and its branches had been a suitable conveyance for her, and now as she stood looking across its rippling surface, anticipation and sadness stung her like a swarm of hornets.

Floating in from the west, high above the Channel, thousands of tiny and brightly colored specks blanketed the sky. They drew closer, hundreds of thousands of burnt orange colored spiders hanging to single strands of self-spun silk, ballooning through the air singing, "It's so nice, to be, a spiiiiiiiii---der. It's soooo nice, to be, a spiiiiiiiiiiii----der. Oh, we spin and spin and never so much as get a grin/it's so nice, it's too nice, to be, s spiiiiiiiiiiiiiiiiii----der/we slink and step, and crawl over all, because we're spiiiiiii-----ders! Eight legs, eight eyes it's nice, to hunt and spy/oh, it's nice, so nice, it's nice, so nice, it's so nice to be, a spiiiiiii-----der!"

A squall that gathered in Brittany sped its way across the Channel; its headwinds pushed across the sea and reached the English side at record pace. The spiders were hit hard and quick; pressed from the grey skies as if a giant cement slab slammed and pushed them to the ground. Some bounced then rolled on the soft sand but most landed on Pi, their thin strands of silk stuck to her feathers from head to toe. They quickly spun more strands, which extended into the cool air. Pi looked like an octopus with thousands of flowing, translucent legs. The silk spinners spun, as the air whipped squalls onto the beach causing the strands to cross and braid themselves into thick ropes. The ropes then braided and crossed until one hundred giant silk arms reached up and out and entwined themselves into massive clasped hands.

"Up, up, up it!" Thousands of tiny voices screeched.

"Red Two?"

"Yes, Red One?"

"Your side is slipping, the thing is not that big or heavy. What's the problem?"

"Not sure sir, but let me adjust my troops."

"Good, get on it toute suite. We've got webs to weave and we need to drop this package off as soon as possible – special orders from way up on high."

"Yes sir! You man there! Pull your line tight. That's it. No, tighter! Good, now the right flank spin long single strands straight out into the wind. Excellent. That's it, keep it up. Hup, hup. Up and hup. Hup-it man, hup-it."

Their collective spinning and pulling and hup-hupping took Pi up in the air in a soft silken basket. Their web engineered so perfectly, so adroitly that not a hole nor seam could be seen. So tightly it was spun to its feathered contents, Pi could not speak nor move the tiniest of muscles. They went about their business of carrying their silent cargo up and out over the Channel bent on accomplishing a mission.

Swiftly they whisked Pi across the vast waters of the Channel. She gave in to the experience and up on any kind of struggle long before they reached the French coast. Knitted into her small silk purse she soared over and through headwinds, floated on thermals and bounced and bobbed along rapids of wind and sleet; over Normandy where Big Fella carried her, down past the beaches where Louise broke her leg and the hill where Pierre dissolved into the chalky cliff side, until the lights of Paris bore through low-lying clouds that ringed the city. Upon seeing her illuminated Paris magnified by the spiders' glossy silk threads, she wept with joy. All the familiar landmarks passed under feet until the center of the world, Pi's world, l'Arc de Triomphe burst through the city's haze like a pulsating star. *Come to me,* it called. *Come to me, I have been waiting for your return.* Avenue de la Grande Armée rose from the ground and reached out like a long spindling arm and grabbed the ballooning arthropods and their payload.

"That's the signal. We're in the drop zone, Pont de Neuilly. Drop, drop it now," Commanded Red One.

"Roger, Red One. Dropping now." But they drifted too far off course, too far southeast and dropped Pi from way up high, way too far for a flightless bird. As she plunged to the cobbled streets below, Red One hollered, "The rest is up to you. Good luck! See youuuuuuuuuuuuuuu......Oh, it's so nice to be a spiiiiiiiiiiiii----der..."

Pi hit the ground with a thud; the silk she was swaddled in unraveled and splayed on a road that pointed towards l'Arc de Triomphe. She stood and looked at her feet, which were bloodied and battered, then back to the spiders who had dissolved into the horizon. She appeared as a tiny speck in a city of millions through the lens of l'Arc de Triomphe. Feeling small and defenseless, avenues de la Grand Armée and Charles De Gaulle seemed out of her reach.

Chapter 18

Piette Phillecroix tidied the nest. Tail feathers swept side-to-side, front to back; side-to-side; front to back; back to front; side to side; repeat. "A busy body is a happy mind," she repeated to herself over and over hoping to calm her nerves and slow her thoughts.

Dr. Allbewell arrived two weeks ago to the day and has been tending to his old friend Paul Phillecroix with expert examination and brotherly care. He had never seen a case like the one that had laid before him. He's had patients with Finch Eye, Septicemia-a-Semitosis, Morgellons, Vulnus Sclopeticum to the head, Feathered Scorbutus, and several sorry souls that succumbed to obitus by Obstipatio Alvi but the weary and waif-like body at his feet had left him baffled and without confidence.

The greater part of last week, Piette Phillecroix spent scouring the City in search of small strands of colored thread. She pecked at discarded bolts of fabric behind second arrondissement garment factories. She clawed through tears and rips in upholstered chairs, rummaged through countless dustbins and would not return home until every available fiber was explored. She gathered everything needed and bound them into small swatches of cloth, tamped them, pecked the family crest onto each and created tiny ribbons. This tradition of finding, gathering and binding thread for the creation of ribbons, has been handed down through the community of pigeons for centuries. The Tossing of the Ribbons Ceremony honors royal and decorated birds many times during the year for those who were about to, or have already, passed on. The ribbons, tossed into the wind, act as a silent alert, informing everyone of important news.

Piette knew that once the ribbons sailed into the wind Paul's fate would be sealed. She dropped a small tear onto the pile of tiny Phillecroix crests and then doubled over in pain. She didn't dare turn to see what was waiting for her. She calmly, almost mechanically, gathered herself and the ribbons and made her way to the edge of the nest. Doctor Allbewell kneeled next to Paul Phillecroix checking his pulse by placing his finely tuned ear next to his heart. Piette stopped at the groundsill, one foot on the sill and one remaining in the nest. She tuned her ear to the slow respiration of her husband's breath. She no longer heard the whisper of life that had emanated from him for all their years of partnership.

Without realizing it, one of the ribbons was snatched by the cool spring breeze and was carried westerly, away from l'Arc.

The tiny speck crossed avenue de Madrid near the Church of Saint Jean Baptiste and grew larger as it dodged cars and motorcycles on its easterly course.

The shimmering scrap of black cloth waltzed to the whim of its unseen dance partner. It twirled and twisted through treetops and windowsill flower boxes, dipped and brushed against freshly sprouted buds on its way to the city streets below.

Pi hobbled towards l'Arc de Triomphe. She came around the place de la porte Maillot and on to avenue de la Grande

Armée. A gust of wind hurtled down the avenue and smacked her to an abrupt halt in the center of the rotary.

"Piette?" Dr. Allbewell gently whispered. She stiffened and stood with her bundle of bows transfixed on the Parisian sky.

"There are many breezes to carry the bows today," Piette said to no one in particular. "It's time to cast these off. One should not neglect one's responsibilities." She didn't dare look at Dr. Allbewell. She couldn't bear to confirm what she already knew. "Keep Paul warm while I'm gone. There's some strewn straw in the corner you can use." With the bundle of bows latched in her beak she hopped with both legs onto the edge of the stone roof. Facing west she alighted onto a tip of the silver metal fence that encompasses the parameter of the roof. Raising her head high, Piette looked into a sea of pink, blue, gray and lavender. As she peered into the aerial painting, her heart shattered into a million pieces that tumbled to the pit of her empty soul. She gasped for breath, as the bundles of bows spilled from her beak and were carried upward to the multi-colored vortex. The swirling colors of the sky churned by the wind grabbed the bows and sent them in every direction. Flying through the air, sailing over the spokes of avenues that make up the place Charles de Gaulle. Dancing in the wind, spinning and rotating like miniature whirlybirds, they traveled north over avenue Mac Mahon and south towards the river Seine. They dipped and soared over tree-lined avenue Foch, turned and took downward spins onto avenue de la Grand Armée.

Piette sent screams of desperation into the winds, "Pi! Where are you?! Come home, please..." She begged the great winds to find her daughter, to bring her home, so that she, Paul and Pi could be a family again if only for a few brief moments.

"Great Bird, I implore you, please bring my daughter home. Please, please."

Crossing rue Duret after being punched by a strong wind, Pi started for home again. A voice passed through the morning wind and as she stopped to listen, a ribbon swept up the avenue skimmed the asphalt, teased gravity until it wrapped itself around her tired legs. She grabbed it in her beak and immediately recognized the family crest. She knew all too well what it meant. She dashed towards l'Arc de Triomphe answering the voice lodged in her ears. "I'm coming mère, I'm coming." But her muscles were unable to match her passion; exhausted she stumbled to the ground. Her left leg torn to the bone, spatters of blood, stained the cement and dizziness filled her head. She collapsed and slammed her head against the hard curb; her body wedged between the curb and a rusted sewer grate.

High above, a strong and fearless bird took flight and coasted on thermals of well-worn paths. Eyes pierced, sharpened claws tucked under his streamlined body, he hunted through the city haze for a morsel, a taste, a meal; his acute hearing tuned into something below. His internal radar locked onto his helpless prey two hundred feet below and killer hormones secreted into his brain. As he adjusted his tail he shot like a speeding missile with wings tucked and beak pointed. Twenty-five feet from his target he lowered his legs and put his claws into the kill position. Just as he was about to strike he noticed a streak of blue folded across the feathers of his victim. He lifted his wings and ruddered himself slowly to the curb above the gray sewer grating. He surveyed the bird at his feet, and again took notice of the blue color running through its chest feathers. A barking pit bull charged up from behind and snapped at him with bared teeth. With a flick of his right front claw he cut a deep scratch across the dog's nose leaving it yelping. He turned back to the injured bird and looked carefully before speaking. "Pi? Pi Phillecroix, is that you?" Nothing…again he tried arousing her by stepping in closer and whispering in her ear, "Pi, it's me. Can you hear me?" In and out of consciousness, Pi's head swelled with pain. Her legs numb, his voice drifted around her ears. He tossed her with the tip of his middle claw and she moaned. Her left eye cracked open.

"Poor little bird." He slipped his strong left wing under her weak body and lifted her up and out of the metal grating dragging her under the frame of a parked car.

"Pi? Wake up, Pi."

Her head rolled left then right; she opened her eyes. "What…who…who are you?"

"It's me, Nicolas Jacquet."

"Qui?"

"Nicolas Jacquet. We haven't seen each other for many years but I was there at your birth."

"I'm sorry, I…"

"It's okay, you probably don't recognize me. I used to be very scrawny."

"Nicolas? Yes, Nicolas Jacquet, I do remember. You have grown into a fine bird. I have thought of you often."

"I know."

"You do?"

"Yes, and along with many others, I have been looking for you. Your père is…"

"My father, yes? What about him, did he? Is he…?"

Nicolas turned away and looked toward l'Arc de Triomphe.

"I have to get home. Please, help me up."

"You're in no condition. I'll fly to your family's nest and let them know that you will be home as soon as you are able."

"Non! I must finish the journey. Please, just help me to stand."

"Ce n'est pas possible."

Pi looked intensely into Nicolas' eyes, the way she had the day she was born. He hadn't known what she had been through these past few months but he sensed what she needed. "There is nothing I can say to keep you from dragging yourself home is there?"

"Non, there is not Nicolas, but I appreciate your help. I want to go home, I need to know…birds like us Nicolas…well, birds like us. You understand don't you?"

"Oui, I understand. 'Birds like us.'"

Nicolas stepped back and let Pi rise to her feet. "I'll see you soon I hope."

"You will, I'm certain of it."

"Do you want me to…?"

She finished his sentence for him, "Non don't. I want to surprise them. Go now Nicolas, we'll see each other again soon, I'm sure."

Nicolas paused and looked at Pi before he leapt. Once airborne, he circled high above watching over her every arduous and painful step home.

Pi's exhaustion was starting to win. As she headed for the avenue de la Grande Armée she became confused and disoriented. She turned right on avenue Alphand towards rue le Sueur where she turned right again placing her in front of an alterations shop. Rue le Sueur was narrow and without traffic. It's grey, beige and white shutter-framed windows looked like outstretched arms protecting and guiding. Straight ahead was avenue Foch; an emerald laced garden of poplars and oaks with tightly trimmed grass laid out like a blanket. "Which way?

Which way?"

She turned left on rue d'Argentine bringing her to the "I" intersection of rue de Saïgon. "Which way? Which way?" She had zigzagged her way until she turned left on rue Rudy that led her directly to her last steps home. The avenue de la Grande Armée, wide and inviting, lay at her pink and bloodied feet. She knew exactly where she was as she turned her head to the right and saw the Place de l'Étoile, its twelve-pointed star stretching out now like rose petals that would carry her gently home. She walked towards it, first slowly with pain, then gradually she began to run until she reached the all too familiar ring of cobblestones that encompassed her home.

This time she walked confidently towards the busy circle of traffic that rung the star. She placed one foot in front of the other. The fast moving cars, motorcycles and trucks were perfectly timed. It was if the machines themselves were part of a choreographed timed dance and Pi was their lead. When she reached the other side she stood at the foot of l'Arc de Triomphe. Her home, her family atop the stone building was only moments away and all of Paris at this moment seemed so foreign and surreal. Tears formed in her small eyes. She had been away for so long and now here she was back in her city, her beautiful city and she knew not what awaited her in the rooftop nest.

Chapter 19

Pi CRAWLED UNDER THE huge wooden door that led to the winding set of endless metal stairs. They appeared larger and longer than she remembered. The first step up was painful and each subsequent hop was labored and more painful than the one before it. Each was matched with a small thud. It was harder than she ever could have imagined. She told herself to keep moving, just ignore the pain; she had endured much worse on her journey; if not for herself then for at least all those who had helped her: Pierre, Big Fella and Louise. She pressed on step-by-step, hop-by-hop until she reached the pinnacle of the swirling stairs and the flat concrete floor just below the rooftop nest. It stretched out before her like an endless grey sea. She took a deep breath and made her way across the floor and to one last staircase that led her to the family nest.

It was precisely three o'clock in the afternoon when Pi's left foot crossed the threshold taking her from lone traveler to reunited family member. Three o'clock. Seconds away from the loving pecks and embraces that she had dreamt of for months. She could hear her father's mournful wheezing and paused to listen to his labored breaths. It devastated her to hear him sounding so weak and frail. She hesitated for a moment then poked her head in slightly to measure the situation. Her father

197

looked like half the bird he was when she left home to search for Dr. Allbewell. Her mother, thin and without hope, stared without expression. Dear, sweet Dr. Allbewell, tended to his patient and his patient's wife. Tears misted over Pi's eyes, which caused her to sniff through her tiny nostrils.

Piette turned and called out, "Hello, is someone there?" Pi lifted her head and walked into full view and when hers and her mother's eyes met, their worlds stopped, rotated counter clockwise, paused, then moved forward again.

"Mon Dieu. Mon Dieu, my baby, my sweet little perfect egg."

"Mère. Oh, mère…"

"Ma chérie, come to me my darling girl."

They embraced and pecked and looked each over to be certain they were both real and together. Locked feather to feather, breast to breast their embrace was stronger than entwined vines of multiple morning glories climbing towards Heaven.

"You have found your way home at last. You are a true blue Phillecroix through and through." Piette stepped back to view Pi from toe to tail. "You have lost weight my dear. Oh, and look at your feet they're bleeding! Step in the straw there and wipe them clean."

Pi dutifully followed Piette's direction and happily received her mother's attention and care. "I've missed you mère, more than I could ever convey." She then turned her head over her right shoulder and saw her father sitting on his legs with his head slumped upon his chest. With straw stuck to the now dried blood on her feet, she slowly walked past Dr. Allbewell who winked hello, and then sat down by her father's side.

"Père? Père, it's me, Pi. I'm here père"

Paul Phillecroix was slow to open his eyes, first the left then the right. They were covered with a thin film of partially dried mucous. He rasped between shallow breaths punctuated by pauses of silence. He turned his neck and looked directly at Pi. She fought back tears knowing that he could not see her.

"Père. My dear courageous and handsome père."

Through a slightly parted beak Paul Phillecroix said, "Pi. My brave flyer has at last come home to roost."

"Pour vous, père."

"Je le sais."

"You know everything père. You taught me everything that is most important about life and living."

"Je suis sûr…" He paused as his lungs groped for air. "I am sure that you could teach me things now…that I never knew. Your perspective is très unique, c'est vrai. Tell me about your journey. Tell me everything. I want to hear…" He made clicking sounds as he started to wheeze and gasp for breath.

Doctor Allbewell rushed to Paul and removed the discharge from his nostrils and covered his eyes with grass. "You'll need to let him rest now." Turning to Pi and Piette he said, "Perhaps later he'll feel strong enough to speak more. Why don't you two go out on the roof for a while?"

"I am not leaving him now, Dr. Allbewell. After all the time I have been away I could not possibly leave him now."

"Pi," Piette said, "Listen to Dr. Allbewell. If it were not for all his efforts your father may not still be with us. Come little bird, let the good doctor, your father, and the Great Bird do their work."

Pi reluctantly followed her mother's instructions and the two went out on to the roof where Piette listened to Pi recount her journey. Piette gasped, then wept as Pi told her all the details, of friends made and lost; the sweet, rich and luscious landscapes she walked along, and the cruelness and wickedness she had witnessed and experienced.

Dr. Allbewell continued throughout the day to apply his poultices, salves, balms and ointments, all to no advantage in improving Paul Phillecroix' condition.

Several hours had passed until he requested for Piette and Pi to come back to the nest.

"Piette, I have done everything I can for him. He's in the wings of the Great Bird now."

Completely frail and just a few breaths from death's door, Paul Phillecroix reached out with one wing and pointed beyond Pi and Piette. Deep in his eyes was a profound passion that bore into another realm well beyond the nest. He reached forward and in a poised and calm voice said with complete confidence,

"It's time to go. I must to go now."

"Go where mon chéri? Where Paul, where do you want to go? Is it to the Jardin des Tuileries my love? To sit upon the stonewall surrounding the pond? Yes, that's it isn't it? Of course it is. That's settled then we shall go to the pond and you will see all of your friends and we can talk and put our faces in the sun and warm our blood huddling close together."

Pi and Doctor Allbewell helplessly watched Piette in her desperation. "Pi, help me get your father ready for travel." Pi stood frozen and confused, numb to the situation. "Pi!" Écoutez! Did you not hear what I said? Help me get your father ready!"

Piette Phillecroix, with all her years of strength and wisdom and family devotion, crumbled. Her love, her life, was never again to sit and chat with his friends by lapping pond waters.

Pi turned to Doctor Allbewell begging for help, "Doctor Allbewell isn't there something that you can do?"

"My precious bird, there is nothing that anyone here can do for your father. He is off to another life now, perhaps better than the one he had here."

"Doctor Allbewell, where else could père possibly go that would be better than here in Paris with his family?"

"Lass, we believe that every living soul goes on to another life after they are finished with the one that they have experienced here."

"Where is this place Doctor Allbewell, and what is it like?

His tone and language shifted to that of scientist and scholar. "No one knows for sure but it's been said that this place is everywhere. It's all around us, and yet, it is not here as we know it. It is beyond description. If I were to tell you that it was beautiful, this would not describe it correctly for there are no words to describe this other place. There's a thin veneer between our lives now and those that are awake and alive in this other world. You see, there are dimensions that we have just begun to appreciate even though we have known about them since the first squab walked the planet."

Pi was trying very hard to understand what the good doctor was telling her but the more he spoke the less she understood.

"It's not important that you fully understand right now, Pi. What's important is that your père will be with you no matter where he is and you with him."

"Doctor Allbewell, I'm sorry but I don't understand. If we can't see this place that you are describing then how do you know what it's like? Have you been there yourself?"

Doctor Allbewell knew that he could not describe the indescribable and maybe in time Pi would come to comprehend and understand for herself. It is believed that every pigeon that has pecked and drank of this life will go on to the next, where they will live without living and be without doing. All the birds that have ever flown and walked before them will be there to greet them. This is the great truth for those that believe it.

"But Doctor Allbewell what are we to do without père? Where shall we live, what shall we do? Did I travel all this way just for you to come here and do nothing?"

Doctor Allbewell tucked his wings further behind his shoulders giving him the look of a small penguin. He waddled close to Pi, took a deep breath and stretched out his wings to encompass her. She shrugged them away and called her mother, "Mère? Do you hear what Doctor Allbewell is saying? Is this true, do you know this place?"

Piette calmly walked toward her. She spoke in soft and warm tones. "Mon chéri," she began. "This is the time that all of us know will come but would like nothing more than to pretend that it will never happen. Your père is dying. This is the process of death and rebirth. He will leave us soon and will go on to live in the place that Doctor Allbewell described to you. This is not difficult nor painful as long as the dying surrender to the death of their current life and have faith and belief in the life they do not yet know."

Looking down at her listless and withered father, Pi's strength broke and she collapsed to the nest floor burying her face in his dry and brittle feathers.

"Pi," he whispered. Look under the straw I have something for you."

Digging under the bed where her father lay Pi pulled out a red and white ribbon with her beak. Attached to the end of the ribbon was a silver medal inscribed with the words, *La medaille d'honneur pour merite, bravoure et devouement a la France.*

"Pi, I want you to have this medal. You have earned it and I give it to you with much pride." She was speechless. How could she accept such a generous gift? She knew how much her father's medals and ribbons meant to him.

"But père, I can't take this. It's yours…I can't …"

"I want you to have it. You have crossed the sea and have returned to the nest. You are the best daughter that a father could have ever wished for. I am proud of you and know that you will carry on the Phillecroix name with pride. You are indeed a rare bird. A very rare little bird indeed. Pi, listen carefully because I want to tell you about one of life's most precious secrets."

"Yes père, what is it?"

"Accept life and everything in it as it is. Acceptance will give you peace and it will give you direction. Acceptance of all things as they are will bring harmony to your soul."

"I don't understand père."

He was wheezing heavily now as it took every last bit of his strength trying to pass something onto his daughter. "You must accept that I will soon be gone and that…"

"No! I don't want to accept this père!"

"Listen to me Pi. When you accept that I will soon be gone…" He gasped for breath as his lungs pounded with pain. "Pi, no matter what you do or where you go I will be with you. Just feel my presence around you."

"What happens père when I need you and you're not there what should I do then?"

"Don't you see little bird that you are all that you need? You have already conquered the greatest challenge that any of us will face in our lifetime."

"What's that père?"

"Yourself my precious child. Yourself."

"What? Père, I don't understand. What do you mean that I conquered myself?"

There was no answer. Paul Phillecroix slowly closed his eyes. A speck, a silver speck that Pi unknowingly had been carrying with her, lifted from her back feathers and settled onto her father's chest. It buried itself deep into his thick blue-streaked feathers and bore into his skin. He shrieked in pain, his chest heaved and his back lifted from the bed. Then he collapsed back onto his soft bed of straw. Shock silenced the room. Time stood still, faces, heads, wings, tails, eyes, feathers; everything paused, frozen in disbelief.

"Père. Please don't go yet. Please!"

Piette and Doctor Allbewell moved to console Pi and as they did Paul Phillecroix' chest rose then dropped. He lay completely still for a few seconds before his head slowly drooped and rested in the center of his blue crest.

Anger and sadness flowed into each other and created more energy than Pi could have summoned otherwise. Her heart pumped massive amounts of blood that flowed to her lungs that pumped massive amounts of oxygen to her brain that forced her wings to flap repeatedly. Piette and Doctor Allbewell watched in amazement as she flapped harder and harder until the feathers on her own and her father's crowns rose from their heads. Paul Phillecroix' crown feathers acted as guide wires and lifted his head up and off from his chest. His eyes still closed, his shoulders lifted from his back as Pi transferred her energy to him until he rose to his feet, opened his eyes and puffed out his chest.

Chapter 20

THE NEWS SPREAD QUICKLY of Pi's return. No one expected her. Stories floated through the arrondissements about her journey, all gossip, of course, "Left dead somewhere," most said. "Il n'est pas possible she could survive for so long so far from home."

After a few feathers of surprise and astonishment fell from their heads, a grand celebration was planned. One that had not been seen since the first Ectopistes Migratorius flew three thousand years ago carrying a message from the Egyptian artist Thutmose to Queen Hatshepsut, asking for permission to redesign the bust of the Queen that he was commanded to create. The mayor, Aleta Pache originally wanted to have the ceremony at the base of l'Arc de Triomphe but its capacity was limited, so she decided that it would be best and most appropriate to hold it at the Tuileries where its lush, green runways could be seen from high above.

When the day arrived thousands had waited in early morning rains to get a glimpse of Pi and Piette. An aged and revered poplar tree was chosen for its ringed base that has been a meeting point for many, many years. It was perched on a small mound surrounded by a sloped incline, painted green as far as the eye could see. Paul Phillecroix anxiously wanted to attend but was still too weak. He convinced Pi, Piette and Doctor

Allbewell to go without him and hid his disappointment and sadness when they left the nest. His disappointment was assuaged when he heard a commotion of birds below the nest that had come to escort Pi, Piette and Doctor Allbewell to the celebration. Madame Jacquet, Pierre, François, Guy, Pascal, and of course, Nicolas were first to greet them when they exited the door at the base of the Arc.

"Pi Phillecroix," Nicolas stately declared, "we the Jacquet family would like the honor and privilege of escorting you to the party, if we may have the pleasure?"

With a slight bow of her head Pi met his eyes and replied, "Monsieur, I would like nothing more than for yourself and your handsome family to walk with me to the Jardin des Tuileries."

Pi, Piette, Doctor Allbewell, and the Jacquet family turned in unison, faced southeast and walked out from under l'Arc. Soon thereafter, The Cambiers, Stephan and Paulette, alighted and joined the walk. Madame Bertin was nursing a head cold but sent along a message with Paulette to be delivered as follows, "Indirectly to the not young longer but still the wisest of the wise Pi Phillecroix, that all is all and all is better now that you have been gone and now are home. Bless you, sincèrement, madame Bertin." It was the last coherent sentence that madame Bertin would utter. She died hours later having choked on her own fluids.

The small troupe of walking fliers made their way down the avenue des Champs Élysées along the same rue that dignitaries, tourists, politicians, kings, queens, lovers and artists, all had walked for hundreds of years.

As Pi walked atop the paved les Élysées she thought of and felt all the souls that had walked before her until one called out and said, "Odelette, you have returned. My dear Odelette, I have missed you so."

The Jacquets and the Cambiers hadn't heard the voice nor did Piette or Doctor Allbewell.

"Odelette, Odelette, come now and see your mére."

This time Pi turned her head completely over her shoulder and noticed Natalie Caron limping towards her and the others.

"Odelette!" She hollered.

"Madame Caron!" Pi yelled back. She ran to her and when they came together tears rolled down from their tiny eyes.

"Madame Caron, I am so happy to see you, if it were not for you I wouldn't be here now."

"Of course you wouldn't, I gave birth to you." Madame Caron paused then smiled seeing the look of disappointment on Pi's face. "Pi Phillecroix, it is so very good to see you as well. That night when we met I knew that it was time to let go of Odelette. You gave me that gift and I am very grateful. May I walk with you?"

"Of course you may, I'd be honored."

As they walked, the avenue became dotted with young and old, tall and short, brown and red, short feathered and long, of each and every bird that lived in the leafy trees, roosted on stone windowsills, and in patinaed drainpipes. All had come to see Pi and as she passed, they flocked to her like spun sugar to a stick; a large mass of meshed feathered colors.

They arrived at the Tuileries at eight o'clock and were escorted to the respected Poplar tree where a small crowd had already gathered. Pi looked out at the sea of birds who at that very moment had raised their eyes skyward. It had darkened with thousands upon thousands of birds about to descend upon the Tuileries. Dignitaries from around the globe had come to honor Pi. The royal Duke of Earle and his beautiful wife Lady Earle had traveled all the way from the British countryside to attend the ceremonies. The highest-ranking emissary of the small town of Perpignan, Don de Manuel Garcia Sebastian Cologne, along with his entire family, landed with all the pomp and circumstance that one would expect from a pigeon of his stature. Senorita Jacobo, the great-great-great granddaughter of Hernán Pedro Jacobo, one of the world's earliest visitors to Paris, was accompanied by her fiancé Don Juan Fernán Lafuente. Every type of pigeon was represented. Leading the way were white bokhara trumpeters with their feet fanned with long tail-like feathers and head feathers that swooped down past their beaks. Following the trumpeters and flying in from Germany were beautiful Jacobins with high collars of black fur that topped their bald heads. Red ribbontail fantails and lahores came from as far away as India. Diplomats were in attendance who represented more than two hundred different breeds of pigeons and other birds as well; all unique in their shape, size and color. Dippers from Ireland looked as if they were baked to perfection in their roasted-honey colored feathers. Kingfishers flew across the Channel with their rich blue underbellies casting a heavenly quilt on the onlookers below. Artic terns sidestepped their twelve thousand mile flight back to the Antarctic just to attend the ceremony. From closer distances, peacocks, adonis blues, heaths, marbled whites, and pearl-bordered fritillary butterflies came to honor Pi and her courage.

Once every tree, shrub and fence post was occupied, the mayor walked to the base of the poplar tree and addressed the crowd. "Mesdames et messieurs, I present the key of the City of Paris to mademoiselle, Pi Phillecroix." As the Mayor continued, a faint sound started its way towards the crowd, steady and constant, "Da-dump dump, da-dump dump, bad-da-da-da-dum dump."

The ground began to rumble as the noise became louder. Everyone looked to see where it was coming from but saw nothing. The Mayor turned from her place above the crowd and spotted something and said, "Look, there!"

"What is it Mayor," her deputy asked. The Mayor couldn't believe her eyes.

"What do you see?"

"Charles, come up here and bring Pi with you."

The Deputy led Pi up to the top of the mound closest to the trunk of the tree and when she turned she couldn't believe what she saw. Never had she seen anything quite so strange and beautiful as what was coming towards her. In all her travels and with all the creatures she had met nothing compared. It was a heavenly procession. Making their way towards the Tuileries living angels wove their way through the shimmering mass. Each member of the procession, unique and special, came into full view of the crowd. Some hobbled on one leg while others limped along with maimed or broken feet, as others were carried by friends or loved ones who came in partial darkness. Young and old, short, tall and different they poured into the park, proud and anxious to see their hero.

When the last wing of feathers fell back into place the crowd hushed and waited until bubbles of whispers rose from the rear of the crowd and floated in the air and popped near an ear here and there. "Look, Paul Phillecroix is here."

"It can't be."

"Did someone say that Paul Phillecroix is here?"

"The fastest flyer? Non, he's gone for ever. I saw the ribbons."

"It cannot be. It just cannot be."

Lying in his nest, Paul Phillecroix could not bear thinking of not sharing his joy and love for his beloved wife and daughter. He had to be with them. If it were not for the easterly winds that carried him directly to the Tuileries he never would have made the celebration. It would have taken too much strength, strength he had not yet recovered.

Upon entering the west end of the park, a slice formed in the mass of birds allowing Paul Phillecroix to walk through the crowd. Tears flowed as he passed. Intimates and strangers alike shared their adulation. Those standing or seated at the front couldn't make out what the commotion was about, but as he walked towards the poplar tree the energy and excitement moved through them like electricity.

Not until they laid eyes on the decorated veteran did anyone believe he was still alive. A middle-aged, rotund, root beer colored bird shouted out, "Parfait! Paul Phillecroix est perfect!" The crowd picked up on the brown bird's cheer and chanted, "Parfait, Parfait, Parfait, Paul Phillecroix!" Over and over and over until their cheers could be heard all over Paris. Their song for the revered flyer was sung from one end of the city to another and then carried across Europe to Asia and south to the Pole and back north; its notes pitched, rolled and yawed from the Paris axis. The crowd formed a long line that swept Paul Phillecroix up in its admiration and carried him towards the Mayor, who was standing with Pi and Piette.

He turned to the crowd and addressed them. "My fellow great birds of Paris and beyond. You honor me with your praise but you did not travel and gather today to see an old bird like me strut about. Non, we are here today to honor and acknowledge the bravest, most heroic, and death-defying pigeon of all time. And I might add, intelligent as well. Mesdames et messieurs, a parent has no greater pleasure than to see his or her child, their only child, grow to be a pigeon that they can be proud of. Pi Phillecroix, great granddaughter of Pipio Pibionem and Paul Phillecroix I is par excellence. She has taught us what we should strive to become. She is a pigeon beyond compare who exemplifies selflessness, grace, beauty and courage. Mesdames et messieurs, s'il vous plaît, welcome the City's number one daughter..." Paul Phillecroix paused trying to hide his emotions from the crowd. "Mesdames et messieurs please flap your wings and welcome the City's number one daughter, Pi Phillecroix."

All at once the loudest sound of wings that have ever flapped in unison, greater than any migration in history, shot out from the crowd. The thunderous appreciation rocked Pi back on her heels. They flapped their wings for what seemed like hours. Every time Pi attempted to speak the crowd got louder. She never imagined that she would be standing here with the love of all of Paris at her feet. The whole of her being became so extraordinarily energized and pure that she became lost in it. Time and space and all boundaries evaporated into this one moment, and a peace that Pi had never known, radiated and glowed from her presence and reflected brilliantly back onto the crowd. The calm and peace emanating from her enveloped everyone causing souls to link and hearts to beat and pulsate in symphonic rhythm.

"Ladies and gentlemen, mesdames et messieurs, vive la France!" The crowd went wild with appreciation and hundreds of birds fluttered their wings lifting them several feet from the ground. The scene from above looked like hundreds of multi-colored marionettes dancing up and down. Once they came to rest in place again Pi continued, "This is the land of my every dreams however, I dedicate all that I am, all that I ever will be to my père and mère, the most wonderful parents that a girl could wish for. They have taught me to listen deeply, to look for the good that is in all of us, to trust, and most importantly, to love.

"No matter who you are..." Pi abruptly paused as a lone bird in the crowd caught her attention. The bird walked slowly towards the front of the crowd, its eyes fixed on Pi. It was a gull and looked familiar; the color of its feathers, its gait, the tuft of red atop its head. Pi recognized her and called out, "Louise! Louise! Mon Dieu, is it really you? I cannot believe that you are...I mean I am so glad to see you!"

The gull did not respond - just kept its gaze locked onto Pi.

"Louise, are you alright?"

"Mademoiselle Pi, my name is Fingal and I am a cousin to your friend Louise."

Pi's heart sank when she realized who he was.

"Mademoiselle, it is with my deepest sympathy that I bring you the news that my dear, sweet cousin Louise has been lifted to the eternal sky."

A tear rolled down her face. "I am so sorry for you and your family monsieur Fingal. She spoke well of you and your family."

"Merci mademoiselle. Soon after you left her in Normandy my family and I heard her call and did all we could to save her, but it was too late. She told us that you didn't want to leave her but that she insisted that you look after yourself. She told us of your urgent plight and how far you had traveled. We are truly grateful for your willingness to help her."

Pi walked closer to Fingal. She brushed her right wing to his left and said, "You are so wonderfully gracious and thoughtful to come here today. You are welcome to stay with me and my family for as long as you wish."

"It is my honor, mademoiselle."

Pi walked back to the high point on the tree mound and continued to address her audience. "Mesdames et messieurs, pardonnez moi. No matter where you have been or have not been; no matter what color your feathers are; whether you have one eye, one foot or just one wing, we are one. We want the same things: to love, to be loved, to be respected; to be secure in our nests and to have clean drinking water and fresh grains to eat."

Fingal had not taken his eyes away from Pi since he arrived. She didn't know it yet but he too had been on a journey, a long journey in search of someone and if the mist in his eyes was any indication, he found what he had been looking for.

"I say to you mesdames et messieurs, ladies and gentleman, we are one. So many beautiful birds stand before me. So many different types of birds but no matter what language we speak, we pigeons have the same name and just for today, all of you dear friends are pigeons.

"In Arabic we are called "Hamam" in Chinese, "Buck Gup" and in Dutch we are known as, "De Duif." To our brothers and sisters who speak Hebrew we are known as,

"Yona" and in Hungarian, "Galamb" in Norwegian, "Due" in Latin, "Columba" in Portuguese, "Pombo" in Romanian, "Porumbel" and to our Russian friends, "Ролубь" and to our northern neighbors of Spain we are called, "Paloma"." Pi turned to Doctor Allbewell and smiled. "My dear friend Doctor Allbewell, I am so indebted to you. You have taught me so very much in such a short period of time. You sacrificed yourself in order to try and save père. He was correct when he called you the greatest bird he ever had the pleasure of knowing. This is what we do for each other, is it not? Of course it is and you are the purest example of giving I have ever seen." She turned back to the crowd. "All of us must work together to be tolerant of others we do not understand, who may look or sound different. Doesn't a checkered bird deserve the same respect as a white dove? Who here could possibly be better than anyone else simply by the color of his or her feathers?"

Winged applause rose from the crowd, and Paul Phillecroix, with half the strength he once had, shouted, "Vive Pi! Vive Paris! Vive Pi!" The crowd joined in honoring Pi and their favorite city until the squirrels in the trees were shaken from their nests.

When the festivities ended, the parade of international visitors left for their respective homes and the hundreds of ribbons that Piette dutifully constructed had been swept away, the streets around the place de l'Étoile were quiet and still. A few motorcycles and taxis scooted the rotary with ease and a man riding a bicycle with a noisy chain clicked along the periphery. It was Dimanche, the last day of the week, and everyone was resting. A few hours later the bakers will watch their breads rise long before the sun makes her appearance. Birds of every type from all over the City will lay snug in the comfort of their nests and most if not all will rise at exactly the same time, awakened by the same internal clock. One and only one will be the first to sing a single note that signals the birth of a new day. They all rise and fall asleep at the same time day and night, but only one will blow the morning's first note. Every day from now until it is time for another to take her place this one bird will have the honor, privilege and responsibility of playing the morning's trumpet. This is the way it has always been and probably always will be.

Epilogue

EXACTLY THREE-HUNDRED YEARS to the day that Paul Phillecroix I cried out "Où êtes vous mère?!" Paul Phillecroix V, husband of Piette and father of Pi, passed peacefully in his sleep. There were no hysterics from Piette when she woke to find her lifeless husband by her side. She rose from their bed of twigs and went out once again to gather fabric that would make up the family crest. She dutifully tossed the ribbons into the wind that alerted the community to the sad news. Some wept for weeks while others were content with the time they had with monsieur Paul Phillecroix V. Pi came to believe that her father floated from one life into another, just the way Doctor Allbewell told her he would.

The strong and caring Fingal Abernothenoths, cousin of Louise courted, and wooed Pi for a full six months until she granted him the favor of walking her along the fountains of the Tuileries. When they arrived at the far side of the park where Paul and Piette used to stroll, a small breeze lifted their tail feathers, which caused them to lightly brush against each other. A warm sensation ran from the tip of Pi's tail to the end of her beak and when the blue streak running through her breast feathers glowed, she knew. She knew that she would soon bring forth a new life, one that would be Phillecroix through and through. She turned to Fingal and said, "It won't be easy you know? There will be gossip."

"Let there be gossip. Being with you will always be easy."

"Oui, let them gossip. Birds like us…" She trailed off and then said, "Birds like all of us."

FINI

"Come to the edge."
"We can't. We're afraid."
"Come to the edge."
"We can't. We will fall!"
"Come to the edge."
And they came.
And he pushed them.
And they flew.

—Guillaume Apiollinaire

Acknowledgements

This book has been an ongoing project since 2005 when a pigeon walked onto an elevated NYC Subway car, waited for the doors to close, rode the train one stop and then walked back out onto the platform.

I am grateful to the pigeons that I have seen and interacted with on city streets and parks around the world. I admire their tenacity, perseverance, intelligence, love, tolerance and the humor they provide. They along with many other flying species have a lot to teach us about fidelity, conservancy, patience and courage.

The original story was to be a children's picture book but I immediately discovered just how difficult writing for young children could be. Besides, something whispered in my ear that this was to be a book for readers of all ages.

I could not and probably would not have completed this book without the help, patience, encouragement and love of my wife Terry Graziano. She listened endlessly to me as I worked out characters, scenes and dialogue. She read and reread endless chapters and 'final' versions of the manuscript and contributed wonderful ideas and extremely helpful edits. Additionally, she was and is a great creative partner, as we share ideas on a daily basis of making the world a better place to live in through the creative process. My beautiful bride did all this while running her own hat design business. Thank you Terry. I love you.

I can't thank artist and graphic designer, Meredith Reshoft, Owner and Creative Director of The Killswitch Collective enough. I am deeply grateful for her time and creative juices and energy that she put into helping me with the cover artwork and for solely putting the manuscript in electronic and paper formats for publication. Meredith's help and patience through endless text, email and telephone calls can only be described as saintly.

Equally, I am indebted to my oldest and dearest friend, Wendy Muldawer for her original edits and years of encouragement. As a special education teacher who teaches creative writing, Wendy's help and guidance was invaluable.

Gratitude also goes to Latesizia Moreau for reviewing my French usage and grammar. A stalwart finisher of projects started, Latesizia spent many days and one long night converting what I wanted to say into French from my creative English.

A big thank you also goes to Gillian Rosheuvel for putting a sixth and final pair of editing eyes on the manuscript. Working around her already full-time schedule, Gillian provided stylistic and grammatical edits that are seen in this final version.

Lastly, I want to acknowledge my departed parents: my father who shared his intuitive nature, witticism and kindness and my mother's laughter and tenacity while living a life with manic-depression. I love and miss them dearly.

About the Author

Bruce Katlin is a writer, painter, woodcarver and avid outdoor enthusiast. He writes a regular blog on his and others' journeys through the creative process. This is his first novel. He is currently working on a second novel. Bruce lives in Taos, NM with his hat designer wife, Terry Graziano.

• • •